THE WITCH OF HOLLYWOOD

D1737273

THE WITCH OF HOLLYWOOD

Manauia Garcia Tellez

For Marisol & Marcos,

because everything is for you

CHAPTER ONE

PRISHA SULE walked her first red carpet at

21 years old.

She thieved the eyes, smiling till her cheeks

swelled and the red of her lips cracked. Everybody

knew she was a witch. They'd known at the shock of

her sinister beauty and forever blasé mood, but

nobody knew of her youth or the sacrifices she made

to get there; the shedding of her borne skin or the

sinful abandonment of her own blood.

They did not know her reasons why or the stories of her wry childhood, but they had all seen the portrait. It had been whispered of—mimicked, copied, praised. Redone in museums, papers, studied in courses, and still, nobody knew the reason why The Witch of Hollywood was painted on the wall of Hal Moulin's 10.8 million dollar mansion.

"Bill, didn't Hal Moulin marry Vivian Astora?"

"Mmhm."

"But, then—why is there a portrait of another woman here?"

"Where?" He asks, though it could not possibly be missed by the eye.

"There."

"Ah," He says. "Right," He says, as if he had not seen it at all.

"Yeah. So why is it here?"

"Not sure. You'd have to ask her that."

"Her?"

"Yep, Prisha Sule—the witch."

"The witch?"

The woman with eyes coated in blood-like liner, velvet draped across her shoulders, and a crystal ball at her chest.

"Prisha…but why Prisha? Why not Hal? Since this was his house—right?"

"Yeah," Bill says. "But Hal won't tell."

"How do you know that?"

He shrugs as if he's asked Hal Moulin himself. "Hal's done several interviews about this mansion, and in each one somebody asks why he has this painting."

"And?"

"And he tells them to 'go ask Sule.'"

"Oh…then I guess I will have to ask her."

Bill smiles, his voice bitter, "Yep, ok. Good luck finding her."

"What do you mean?"

He saunters into the next room, shuffling through stacks of stale papers that Dustin will sign soon, but not before she pries some more, because mother raised her this way—to be persistent in her wishes, to demand answers if they are not given in will.

"Bill. Doesn't Prisha live in the hills, too?"

"Nope. She used to, but she left the exact year she would be nominated for a Grammy."

"But where—? Where'd she go?"

"I don't know."

"I'll look it up."

"You can't. Nobody knows where she lives now, and if they did, they wouldn't be able to get an answer out of her."

Ever since Dustin Bloom was a kid, she always did what people said she could never do. That's why she was buying Hal Moulin's house, and that's also why she spent three and a half months tracking down The Witch of Hollywood.

Solana is a three and a half hour drive from Los Angeles. The land is hotter there, the sun never shy nor subtle. The beaches are made of browned sand and the streets brim with scents of herbs and ciphers. At first, Dustin Bloom thinks she's in the wrong town, at the wrong house, standing before the wrong woman.

"Hello," She says. "Goodmorning."

"Morning," The woman replies, and she is just as youthful as she is aged. And gorgeous. That cannot be ignored.

"Does Prisha Sule happen to live here?"

"She does. Who's asking?"

"Me, I'm—my name is Dustin Bloom. I'm an agent with Hyatt Blues in North Hollywood and I was wondering if I could speak with her. For just a moment. I have a question."

"A question—about what?" The woman tilts her head, the sharpness of her jaw showing bluntly.

"Uh—about a portrait. It's regarding—an art piece."

The woman does not nod or speak, but steps aside and flits a hand gingerly. Dustin can see the house now, all of it. Its thick windows and long lived plants. Books and rawly peeled fruits.

"You can come on in and wait. I'll make us a smoothie."

Dustin follows, eyes flickering from one thing to another.

"How does oat milk and berries sound? Do you like almond butter?"

"Yes, that...sounds perfect...thank you."

The ceilings are high, and there are windows up there, too. Books are torn, leafed through by starved eyes and hands. Bunches of ribbon are strung across the sofas and letters lie in piles with their ink graying.

"Do you need any help? Making the smoothies, I mean."

The woman lifts her shoulders and grins, "I use a molcajete instead of a blender, so it takes a restless hand."

That is enough for Dustin to cross the room and roll up her sleeves.

"Alright."

"So," The woman says. The corners of her lips turned up, eager almost, "Your question?"

"You're Prisha Sule," Dustin says, because at this point, it is easy to assume so.

"Yes," Prisha smiles, and it is almost bashful. "I am."

"Right. I'm here because I'm buying Hal Moulin's home. So of course I've seen the portrait he has of you and I want to know—"

"The portrait?"

Prisha stops, turns.

The berries lie limp and crushed murderously in her palms. It is then that Dustin is reminded of the portrait. Of The Witch. Of the blood-like art.

"Yeah…the one that takes up his entire foyer wall."

"Is it—it's a portrait of me?"

"Yes."

"What does it look like?"

"It's big," Dustin says, and her voice kneels as Prisha's rises. "And beautiful."

The two women face each other. Prisha has gone silent, and it seems as if the whole world has gone silent with her.

"It's you, as a witch. With a crystal ball in your hands. And you look happy—mysterious, too, like you're smiling at something the artist said. Like an inside joke. Or a secret, maybe."

Prisha nods. Nods, nods, nods. "Go on."

"You were wearing a bell-sleeved top. Your hair was red. Dark red, and ironed straight. This portrait—it's humongous. Like, giant…I'm not sure what else to tell you. It doesn't say who painted it. All I know is Hal won't tell anybody why he has it. He said we have to ask you."

"He said that?"

"I…yes, I believe so. In interviews. In many of them."

"How…interesting." Prisha shifts, wraps her arms around her waist until her back is to Dustin and a crackling sound erupts from the chimney.

"Yes, it is," Dustin glides her palm over the molcajete, lifts the top and goes on crushing oats because she has never found comfort in silence. "So, *do* you know why he has a portrait of you in his house?"

"I do," Prisha says. Then, "I think I do."

She returns to the table, pours the oat milk into the molcajete, and lifts her shoulders again for a shrug.

"It seems he was in love with me."

Using the short rock, she crushes it all. Pounds the fruits till the liquid swirls and shades of purple vanilla mingle bewitchingly.

"Well, that makes sense."

"It does…Hal and I were co-stars once. When we were twenty years old—twenty one, and we worked together when it was a choice and when it wasn't—but then we had our differences—and we didn't see each other for so long."

"Because you left?"

"Partly. But no," She smiles. "Because a three hour drive never stopped anybody."

"True."

"And then I told myself that if Hal ever loved me back, there would be a sign. But when you're in love with someone, everything seems like a sign, so I was specific. I wanted a *real* sign, an obvious one. A big, grand, *art piece*. I wanted a portrait. So there you have it."

"Wait, wait, wait, you've been in love with Hal Moulin since you were twenty one years old?"

"Oh, god no. I've loved Hal for far longer than that."

"But from what I read online you met each other at twenty two years old on the red carpet and *then* worked together on-set a whole year later."

"Yes, but I loved him before that. Long before that."

"How long, exactly?"

Prisha considers this, her face softening where it has honed. In her mind, there is the crackle of a radio, the spright flash of a camera.

She looks at Dustin, takes in the wideness of her eyes, and wonders if there should be trust here. If she should tell her what she knows.

Through the years Prisha has learned to be diligent with what she shares, but she has also learned there can be no secrets for the famed.

As Dustin waits, Prisha makes her decision. She takes two cantaritos and places them on the counter, splitting the smoothie.

Together, they sit on the sofa. One woman on the right side, the other on the left. Then, Prisha begins to tell Dustin the story of how she became known as The Witch of Hollywood.

Dustin Bloom quickly learns that everything Prisha Sule has ever done in her life was for Hal Moulin.

★⁺₊★ ☾ ★⁺₊★

Hal Moulin was born in Paris, his father a french drunk and his mother a secret poet. Her name was Haleena Mei Moulin, a well known Asian American bombshell who cherished her family above the air she breathed. She passed away when Hal turned fourteen years old.

A short time later, at just sixteen, Hal starred in an American film called *The Sailor's Siren.* The distribution was slow, showing at only three modest theaters, but after five months of its release, Lucy Von Rage drove past a billboard with Hal's face on it; the word '*Siren*' drawn in thick, cracked charcoal across his forehead.

With his mother's crimson lips and father's auburn curls, Lucy proclaimed him America's next star. And what Lucy says, goes.

When Hal turned eighteen, he walked the red carpet. I remember this first. I remember this before everything else.

I remember the ache in my ankles and the warm throb of my legs. I remember the chants falling to hushed tones and the people beginning to push with a desperateness. I remember knowing it meant that he was here. It meant he had come, *finally*.

Dust clung to my scarf, and beneath the fabric, sweat dripped in the crease of my neck and the bend of my elbow. I was on my tiptoes, my breath coming fast, and wishing, wishing, wishing, that he would pick me. We were all missing school or work, money or education, all so that we could see Hal Moulin walk past us. And when he did, he did so emotionlessly. Carelessly. But beautifully.

It is known by all that your scarf should never be removed in public. It was forbidden six years before my birth, but the moment Hal began to walk, I felt my fingers itch with a longing. Pulse with an eagerness to tear it from my head.

I found that nothing in the world could bring me to miss a single sound Hal made or a fragment of his face. I would have shed the scarf then my own skin if I had to. I would be bare and held back by nothing just to see and hear as much of him as possible.

I had learned long ago that beauty was a curse, but never more had I wished for it, because beauty held grand, rare privilege. To be loved by Hal Moulin was to be beautiful.

CHAPTER TWO

I was named for the meaning of the fruitless word, *Prisha*. 'Gift of God', though my parents believed in lesser powers and decided I was the effect of well deserved karma. At a young age I was told that this was the reason for my straight hair and plain face. Born cursed, so I would swell easily in the heat and my words would make faces go dull.

I would be quiet and agreeable.

Liked, never loved.

But I did not want to be liked. I wanted to be adored. Praised and pleased. I wanted to see my body and feel vain at its sight. To be like the sirens and nymphs when they flowed past a silver of glass, prideful at the vision.

It was all I thought of—when my head was craned or my lips were bitten, I was thinking of this. Of beauty.

And I was not beautiful.

I had lived my entire life ignored—invisible to my family even, and especially to men. At first I did not mind it. I cherished the ease of sitting at the trunks of trees without bother and swaying while I walked and never hearing any whistles for it. But then I would remember Hal, and my yearn for beauty was a roar in my chest like a lion before feast. I would remember my desperate yearn to be a match, an equal, *an option*—to Hal.

I knew him first by his voice. It came from the sputter of a radio.

"I understand it's their job, I do—"

"Right."

"They're playing a part like I am, but to come to my house at night is…it does not feel appropriate."

"You knew the industry would be like this, though, didn't you?"

"Intrusive, yes, but at some point the cameras go away. Don't they? They're supposed to go away."

He was angry, but not in the ways I had known you could be. He spoke his mind and told his truths, but low and merciful like a mother bear to its most nervous cub. It is the reason I stirred in my seat and asked his name, for the boy who was so obviously unrivaled. But the man who owned the radio frowned and flicked the station to another. Cursed me for being so nosy and unwanted.

He made me angry, and not in Hal's careful way, but in the way of red hot skin and curled fists. The way my parents had shown me.

I was raised on the Eastside of Rey by Morelia and Asim Sule. They worked long hours in factories and drank darksome coffee to keep themselves afoot. They'd been born into orphanages with brutish rulers that called them by ethnicity. My dad was "the Arab" and my mother, "the Mexicana". They had not known intimacy nor kindness, so I never blamed them for their ways.

Until I did.

It was a sound I knew well.

A cry, powerless and bold, stealing me from my sleep. I would have known it even on my deathbed, and it came from the room my small brother slept in.

I had felt my parent's strike before, their curt words and spurned touch. But Benji was 5, and I, 9. There was no hesitancy in me, no thoughts. I only felt desperation in those moments of his pain. I raced like inferno and wailed like a prideful crow with its feathers being picked. They turned to me, their ill-lit faces angered, and I flaunted the marks my nails could make on flesh until they let me take him into my arms.

They never hit Benji again, and they never really spoke to me again, either.

We've lived in the same house in East Rey since then. A place where the streets are built of dirt. Where the air is thick, filling our lungs even at the fall of rain.

Every house here is made of reclaimed wood and brightened with bulbs discarded by the rich. Most of our neighbors knew one another, but they preferred to speak English. They thought it would bring them honor, and my parents did not, so I was the one sent to answer their calls.

Marga passed our house often, leaning her arms over our gates and yelling for me to come out only so that she could tell me of the other neighbor's stories of tragedy and shame. I had listened at first, and then I did not, simply nodding and frowning in some moments, making a smile in others.

Janilah walked past our house to get to her own—it was Janilah I heard most about. She had skin like my own, brown and bright, with a thinner face and higher drawn brows.

The neighbors spoke of her with their lips puckered as if they'd eaten an unripe lime. I had grown used to their talk, but found myself asking still, *what made her so horrible?* But all they did was shake their scarfed heads. They said I was foolish to ask this, and I was, because I saw the envy in the plain of their faces, knew their jealousy like it was my own. They would have fallen ill for a face as silken and slim as Janilah's, given their scraps and knelt before a sorceress for a smile like hers.

But even then it did not make sense. They cherished beauty. They loved Manhuel. He was seventeen and respected for his looks, treated as if he was righteous for having a bronze head of hair and light-colored eyes. Most of the women in East Rey called him *Cariño*, and Janilah was called *Bruja.* I saw this and knew what would become of my name, but it did not matter to me then.

I am nineteen years old now, and God knows, *never ignored*. When you are beautiful—by the standards of society, you are sworn to be both worshiped and slandered. Both loved and loathed. It is said you cannot be one without the other.

My birthday was on the 28th of September. It was the day of the rumor, another day on school campus. I was said to be a skank and Nayeli Polen hated me.

First it was the blue-eyed boy in my second period class who said it. He was sweet-toned and whispering as if he was doing me a favor telling me this. Then it was a girl named Miller, with a more accusing voice, but this time I told her I had not known Nayeli. It was the truth. Maybe she was a peer in a classroom once, or one of the neighbors, but we had never been introduced. And anyway, at the time of the rumor, I was still in my quiet, innocent relationship with Megan Durcal.

We met in the school bathroom outside of the creative arts building. She was a year older, and taller. All legs. Green framed glasses and bruise-like under eyes. I did not think anything except "*baby*" when I saw her, because the professor next door had 'Tossin & Turnin' on loop the entire morning by the plea of her students. The track had just begun again, the door left open, and the sudden guttural croon of Bobby Lewis came again, "*bayyyyyybeee*".

We dated for 4 months. Never met outside of school and never went on dates. Only sometimes would she run a thumb along my jaw, and only sometimes, maybe twice, would I blush.

There was no viable explanation for Nayeli's rumor, and so I smiled to myself and felt relief flush in the pit of my stomach. I now knew with a certainty that the beauty I attained was enough to be both adored and hated for it.

My mother would ask, in crueler tones, how I'd grown so quickly and made my hair twist in glorious ways, and I would try to tell her about last summer, about the days I spent thinking beneath the trees. But she would never stay long enough to listen to what I'd done. How I had cast my scarf away and laid on the lush of the grass, shutting my eyes. Megan used to scold me for this, warn I'd be whipped or fined if I were caught, but I shed them anyway. I do not think I ever saw her without a scarf, but her hair was said to be black as a raven's beak, and I imagined it often, piled around her thin figure, dark and daunting as the rest of her.

It was one of those sweltering afternoons when they began to realize I had changed. My neighbor Henri walked the dirt road that faced our house, wrinkled his nose and said, "You got so tall."

I was barefoot, wearing my thinnest scarf and standing on the flattest ground.

"I'm only 5'7," I said, and knew my pride could not be deterred. 5 '7 was my goal height, and I had just reached it.

"Well, the neighbors on Andap Street said it, too, you know."

"It's just that you're short, Henri," I said, and grinned. "That's why you think I'm so tall."

After that first comment, there were many more. One after the other, each as blunt as the last.

"Your hips are just too curved."

"Why are you always smiling like that?"

"Your waist is so small, it looks creepy."

"You act like you're confident."

"You're just too—too much."

I wrote it all down. I wrote, *It is obvious that I am confident, Mary said so. She said I look taller now too. I am exactly five feet and seven inches tall. I am slim and lean but my hips are wide. People ask me all the time why I always look so happy, and it is because I am.* I wrote this even when it did not feel like the truth, even when I had just wept about the way my stomach welled or my cheeks sunk. I would take the pencil and write more. *Renald said I look five years older than I am, but he said this because I am so womanly and beautiful. I am said to be the embodiment of femininity.*

Other than being a "skank" by the word of Nayeli, a girl I still had not met, I had become known all over campus as "Muñeca". It was the first pleasing nickname I ever had. Megan frowned whenever she heard it, but secretly, I saw the light of her eyes bloom with a limber pride. My own did the same; I had earned myself this name.

I woke every morning before the sun rose, the sky still feeble and gray. I stood in the kitchen crushing half of a cherry between my lips and dabbed the tips of my pruney fingers onto my cheeks, making myself a blush. After school, at each fall of night, I was sure to pluck the small hairs beside my eyebrows to keep their shape. But my eyelashes were the real reason I was called Muñeca. I drenched them in churned oils overnight and coated them in ink by morning. They were long and unnatural and dramatic, but the truth is, I liked looking like a doll.

Where we lived, our faces were most important. They were all you could see; the rest of our bodies were forever covered in heaps of fabric, because of course, the poor must differ from the rich. Only they could show themselves and display their lean figures and diamond rings. They were featured in movies naked or wearing what they pleased, and they did this with the whispered aim of continuing to live off of a hierarchy based on appearance.

They had done this, too, through platforms online. I was nine years old when social media vanished. The people were left in a confusion, thinking it to be a trick of the government.

They had already taken our freedom of expression through hair and clothes, why not our voices, too? But it was not the government, it was the entertainment industry themselves. Money was being made too quickly, too simply, and people were earning fame too easily. So now we are left again with actors and singers for famous figures, but their talent mattered less than their skin. I thought of this day and night, cursing people for their shallowness beneath my breath, and yet fed into it like no other.

Megan broke up with me that winter. She had her hands on the back of her head, her full, red lips cracked with the cold, eyes haunted with the shadows beneath them.

"I don't think you want to be with me anymore."

"What?"

"I think you want to be with someone else."

My cheeks flushed with guilt, my voice coming out higher-pitched than usual. I was quick to defend myself. "I do like you, though. I do. Or else I never would have—"

Megan rose, her legs extending before me, and glared. It was enough for my words to fall limp and fat in my throat. She had always been feisty and more dominant than I.

"That letter you sent me," She began, and I quickly thought of all the letters I had written. They were done in my boredom, on the lines of school paper. "It has somebody else's name on it."

"What are you talking about?"

"Hal."

My eyes grew in their size.

"It literally says *dear Hal*."

Shit.

Megan nodded, lowering her eyes menacingly, as if to say, *exactly*. I said nothing, and instead wondered what would happen if I did not reply. If I said nothing. Ever.

I placed my hands over my thighs and did so.

"Who the hell is Hal, Prisha?"

What if I just keep sitting here stupidly, looking around and shrugging my shoulders? But Megan did not move, only stared, thin eyebrows narrowing over the heart of her face.

She would not leave without an answer, even if it was a reply made in cowardice or shame. She just could not stand to be the fool.

"Hal Moulin," I said, my voice a purr. "You know…the actor."

"Oh, God, Pris," Her shoulders fell from their tenseness. She seemed to be relieved. I almost told her she should not be.

"Really?"

I nodded, "Yeah. Really."

For the last two months, I had been writing to Hal more than Megan. I would be telling her a secret, an observation even, and suddenly the sentences became Hal's, for Hal only.

The first thing I ever wrote to him came from a weeping, frustrated part of my mind. *They care about me like they care about you,* I wrote that I knew they would. I told him how I'd known. *Because it is the same reason the world first fell for you.* I wrote again, *first. First, first, firs*t, because although it was his beauty that drew the eye, it was his talent that kept them. He could cry on demand, and not just simple tears and gasps. Hal broke. His eyes rimmed and swelled, eyebrows tightened across unflawed skin. It is pure sadness to see him cry, and every time, I wept with him.

The second thing I ever wrote to Hal was the beginning of it all. I wrote, *they say I could be in the movies,* and felt my eyes ache, so dramatically proud and angry at once. *One day, I think I will be, just so that I can work with you.*

Megan forgave me and only days later, the school's Theater department asked me to audition for *Peter Pan*. I was set to play Wendy. Everybody knew Wendy, brunette and sweet, with a doll's build and potent innocence. But I was tall and brown and had breasts as well as a bottom. I was studying Psychology, but I took the role anyway and let them dye my hair a golden brown. I told Megan first, and she broke up with me for a second time.

"You're leaving me," I said, and winced at the sound. There was no hurt or desperation, and the words were blatantly dull without it.

"No, Pris," Her shoulders seemed to cave. I was sure it was the first time I had ever seen Megan sad. "*You're* leaving *me.*"

I did not ask her what she meant, but I think she knew. I think she was the only person who ever knew what I would become.

I told Benji second. He had just turned fifteen.

"Really?"

"Yes."

"Are you sure?"

"Yes, I can pull it off."

He nodded, as if he knew this, and I felt more sure of it than ever.

"Will you make money?"

"For what? The acting?"

"Yeah."

"Soon," I said, even though I had not yet thought of it. But I did at that moment, for Benji's sake, and knew I would get myself to earn a pay for it. "Yes, I will."

"Really? Because we need it."

Benji, even as a child, is the bluntest person I have ever known. He gets his indelicate voice from my father and choice of words from my bluff mother. So I should have known what her response would be.

"No pagué. No pagué por el tinte," I said this so she would be less fretful. But she said nothing and I let my fingers drift through my hair for a hindrance. Even with the chemicals, their ends never dried.

"...The school did."

She blinked at me. "Pero estás allí para obtener un permiso en Psicología, no?"

"Si. I *am* there for Psychology, but lately—"

"Dos años, Prisha," The soap bar skidded from her grasp and onto the silver of the sink, still holding the prints of her fingers. "Llevas dos años estudiando. No puedes simplemente cambiar de tu estudio. No ahora."

She looked me in the eyes then. I could see her lips turning to a slit, blenching. *"¿No has oído lo que les sucede a las personas que siguen carreras en las artes? Serás muy pobre, más pobre de lo que somos ahora."*

"No voy a cambiar mis cursos. I was just telling you because—"

She walked away and did not speak to me for weeks.

But I was as good of an actress as I was beautiful.

I would have claimed it was natural skill like the crude flow of a poet, but that would have been a lie. For the past three years, I had practiced without the intention of doing so. I visualized constantly, and my every thought conjured emotion. The crinkle of my eyes, the lines beside my lips for a smile, the scrunch of my nose before laughter. Every spare minute of my life—and there were many without Megan—I sat in the brush beneath the trees and breathed deeply. I thought of who I would become, who I wanted to be, and smiled all the while.

In my mind, I had grown tall enough to brush the leaves of the trees if I went on the points of my toes. I was 5'7, taller than my parents and neighbors. I was beautiful in the ways young girls longed to be.

There was nothing Prisha-in-my-mind could not have. Not even Hal. They made sense—equals in both soul and body. Both sophisticated and adored and successful and held a rareness of mystique that other celebrities could only wish for.

I embodied this version of Prisha mentally, and then suddenly, my skin left its dryness in desolation and took on an unflawed, sheeny base. My chest grew, my nose fit my face kindly, and my jawline was sharper than any man's. I found myself becoming calmer and quieter; I valued my voice, its tone and prudency, and knew some did not deserve to hear what I had to say. This is how my enigma would first become known.

On weekends I walked the dirt roads till I met a sunny patch of land. Most people spent their Saturdays and Sundays in rest, fanning themselves with discarded sheets of paper, laying their bodies across small living rooms, but I was on a hill somewhere with sandals made of old fabrics and Papà's long shorts. I took off my scarf because nobody was around, and it made me feel free. But more than free, I felt *rich.*

Only the upper class could remove their scarves. And up on that hill, I was one of them.

Benji came with me when he had no school work. He laid in the grass with his eyes shut and listened to me talk about films with Hal Moulin in them.

"Pris."

"Yes?"

"You talk about Hal Moulin a lot more than you talk about Megan."

I sat up, brushed my hair from my eyes and said, "Who told you about Megan?"

"I saw you together at school. A while ago."

"Oh."

"Do you like Hal more than her?"

I didn't know Hal, that was the miserable truth, and even then it was more. Far more.

"I like him more than everyone—except for you."

I reached over and fussed at Benji's hair. He shoved me away, held his stubby fingers over his head and yawned for the third time.

"Want to hear about The Sorcerer, now?"

His face went bright. "Yeah."

"Would you rather hear how she grew taller than the Sequoias or how she found the crystals in Mount—"

"The Sequoias!"

I told him about the mantras, the bronzed trunk that spills the tears of a youthful Aphrodite, and the Kundalini awakening. He sat up beside me, stretched like a tensile cat and grinned as I spoke. It was the only way he would hear a lesson, if there was a story at its surface.

"Will this make me as tall as the Sequoias?" He asked, putting his toes on their tips as he stood. "Will it?"

I kept myself from laughing and said, "Yes, yes it will, but make sure to say her mantras before bedtime. You'll be sure to grow if you do both."

"But how?" He asked, and I had my answers.

Benji was not gullible like the other children his age. He needed to hear a voice that did not waver. Opinions were not enough for him, and neither were my stories.

The week after, we found ourselves on another hill, but it had rained and the only place without dampness was beneath a wilting tree. We gave it the name "Floof", for its overgrown fluff of branches and leaves that were velvet in touch.

Benji sat beside the trunk, his face one of anger. "We should leave."

"Why?"

"I can't lay here. There's no sun and it's too cold."

But I was distracted by Floof. I watched as it swayed and hummed above our heads. A branch had snapped, torn at its middle and half drifting toward the ground, a drool of gold coming down with it.

"Look…Benji."

"It's going to rain again. I can feel it."

"Look, Benji, it's honey."

I stepped up from where I knelt and caught the honey in my palms. There was no fear in me, though there should have been. We'd never owned honey, never held a spoon of it to our drying mouths.

Benji rose beside me, stuck his tongue out like the foolish child he had never shown himself to be.

"Wait," I hissed. "Let me try it first."

"Why?"

"To be sure it's okay to eat. You can't just eat random things in the woods. Remember those berries?"

He made a face to mock me. "I thought you said to always *follow your intuition*."

I frowned and opened my mouth for a retort but the honey brimmed above my hands, over my skin and onto the mush of grass and branches.

"Try it," Benji said. "Hurry."

I brought my lips to the thick liquid.

It was not like butter. It had a filling kind of sweetness.

"Go ahead."

Benji stepped past me, opened his mouth below the stream. He liked it more than I and drank till his stomach curved beneath the blue of his shirt.

We bent leaves into cup shapes and filled them with the last of the honey. We thanked Floof and thanked the bees. Benji bowed and shut his eyes. I did the same, but for a moment I stopped to watch as his cheeks pushed out, more so than usual, and he whispered words of gratitude. I grinned, and he must have sensed me staring because his eyes opened and his arms flew out to swat me away.

I returned to that tree for weeks. Crushed older leaves into flakes and used the bendy ones for bowls. The rocks served as feeble knives and the branches for spoons that would be filled with the sweat of summer trunk. I drank and mashed and mixed till oils were brewed with scents that would bring us a calmness.

"Here, drink this."

Benji moved away, hastily, but was not steady on his feet.

"Fu—no."

He had begun to use curse words and I pretended not to hear them.

"Why?"

"Mmmno."

He stared at the green of the tea, making himself more repulsed at its sight.

"Come on, Benji," I whined. "Hold the cup. Think of something you want. Drink it, and you will have it."

"How?"

"With intention, of course. Now drink it."

He drank, we bowed to Floof, and another week passed us by. I was bunching dried leaves and sticks together, binding them by a slim leaf of grass when Benji came and asked for more of the intention tea. I knew it had worked then, and we began to brew.

Benji said I was his closest friend, and though we were bound by same blood and bone it might have made no difference, but he was my closest too, and it meant more to me than anything else.

This was not enough, though, for us to hangout during school hours. Benji stayed with a group of boys, all shorter and giddier than him, and I had Megan. But there were times when we might have taken one break together or nudged each other in the halls in passing. But on Monday we decided to share lunch. It was then that I felt regret larger than I felt pride.

Everything I ever taught Benji was embedded with goodness—never harm. But I doubted myself that day.

"No more berries. They get all…soggy."

"I like them that way. Megan does too. Right, Meg?"

Megan's eyebrows raised, the look one of indifference. She still had the same blueberry in her mouth, rolling it over the edges of her teeth. "*Sure.*"

"She doesn't," Benji said.

"That's not true, she's eating one right n—"

"You're Prista."

We did not have to turn to see who spoke. The boy stood before us. His shadow darkened our faces, the sun holding such a boldness that his brown head of hair went golden with it. "Aren't you?"

I felt Megan tense beside me, the sleek strands of hair falling forward as she beckoned her head to see his face.

"Prisha," She corrected, voice defiant.

The boy's eyes slunk from mine to Megan's. "*You're* Prisha? You don't look like a whore." But then he looked back to me and said, "*You* do."

The boy bled.

Right then, he blinked, and a rawness puddled below the freckled skin of his nostrils. The blood did not slide or fall or drip, it just stayed there.

I heard a gasp. Then laughter. My own gasp next.

"I…"

Megan covered her mouth as she laughed. She rarely did. I turned to watch, already in a sort of awe for the achingly natural beauty she held. Megan had not imagined herself this way—never dreamt of ample lips or appreciated arched brows. Rather she thought it to be more of a curse to be so beautiful.

I might have joined her in this glee, but I was too distracted by the vicious shake of my hands and the tightness at my throat. I lowered my eyes so they were not wide and obvious. In my mind, I saw the boy's smugness, his liveliness. No signs of sickness. *Had I done this?* The quick turn of his lips. The blood that went unmoved. *Had I*—I looked back to Megan, to the boy, and then—Benji.

He bit into the apple I had packed for him, its skin lightly bruised like the boy's nose. He was not grinning like Megan, and there was no shock in his face—only focus. In the dark of his eyes, there was a decision.

"What the fuck."

The boy lifted a palm to his face. His eyes grew and his fingers trembled while he patted himself hurriedly, spreading the blood across the flaxeness of his skin. He cursed again, and Megan's laughter rang sweetly in my ears, but I was still watching Benji.

"The bell rang," Benji said, and left. Megan patted my palm, "Look, Pris. Look. What an idiot. That's what he fucking gets."

I coughed and made myself laugh.

We never spoke of it, Benji and I, but only because I never saw his eyes go so dark again, and I never saw him look so determined either. We kept spending our days on the grassy hills telling tales of manifestations.

Years later, I would wonder how beauty could have brought such peace. I was not always a happy child, but during those years I had become one. Nothing in my life had changed, not really. I only caught myself thanking more of the Earth's goodness, not just the tree we called Floof, but for the nights that granted warmth without a fire, for Benji's health and presence, for the scarves Papà left on my bed when a cent could be spared. For my free education, for living in the same century Hal did, and for all the good I dreamt was to come. In those moments of gratitude, I allowed myself to forget the poverty. To forget the infamy of the people we were kin to. I had assumed that with immense beauty would come fame, and so it did. That year, I learned what Prisha says, goes.

After Wendy, I played Donna in *Mamma Mia*. They dressed me in denim overalls and a floral long sleeve.

There, in the crowds of the young and old, was Lucy Von Rage. The fairy godmother of all agents. She was the only woman in the room without a scarf, and so the room held a dense air spirited with expectation.

The first thing she ever said to me was, "I heard they cast an Indian girl for Donna and now I know why."

I did not even think to correct her, the only thing I saw was opportunity, and the beaming blue of her eyes. I stuck my hand out and grinned proudly the way Prisha-in-my-mind would.

"I'm Prisha Sule." *You know Hal,* was all I could think. *You've shaken Hal's hand, too.* "You're Lucy Von Rage."

"Yes, and you've got a perfect stage name."

"I guess I won't have to change it, then."

Lucy smiled at this and I was pleased. Most people frowned or cackled at the certainess of my words, but not Lucy. She knew the power of it.

"How old are you?" She asked, and the applause had begun to halt. They all wanted to hear, and I did not blame them.

"Eighteen."

I would be 21 years old in a few months, but I had read enough articles on the importance of newly borne skin and a girlish voice. It is what the people want: the young and pretty.

"Perfect. I want you to come to an audition tomorrow morning on Sunset Boulevard. It's not for another play, but a movie. Just read the script and see what happens, alright?"

"A movie," I smiled. "Alright."

"Do you think you can make it?"

"I'll be there. I wouldn't miss it."

Lucy left then.

A perfect line of ground went empty for her parting. The other students followed at her heels, blinking with eyes of longing that did not show any attempts for subtleness. I watched, trying to keep my eyes on her practiced sway, but instead I noticed how nobody else was bid hello or sought out, and felt guilt as well as gratitude.

I had worked with the students in the Theater department for months and heard their goals spoken of enough to feel as if they were my own. *Maybe they weren't practicing enough,* I thought. *Or maybe they just weren't dreaming hard enough.*

Rene, the senior who played Sophie, came to me right then. Her scarf sagged below the dark brown of her curls. This was how I knew she suffered, enough that she let herself forget the law.

"I've been waiting for Lucy Von Rage to scout me for years," She did not smile with praise or pride, instead her lips were set downward, curved with hurt and tire. "I knew it would never happen."

Ah, I thought. *That's why.*

★⁺₊★ ☾ ★⁺₊★

Prisha Sule auditioned for the role of Marietta on November 17th. She walked in with the sort of lips shown in cosmetic ads and a green scarf that had already lived many years. Marietta wore pink every day, from head to toe, it didn't matter the shade, and carried her poodle everywhere. Each and every member of the casting crew looked past Prisha. They saw only the color of her skin and a faded scarf. But Prisha wanted the role, and that's all that mattered.

I had pink hair that whole year. It was light as if dipped in cisterns of sand shells and curled at its ends. The look was aimed for an old fashioned ad. I was a school dropout by summertime and worked on-set as Marietta all day. I came home one evening, the sun well within the clouds, and told Mama I was leaving. She had not even looked me in the eye as she said, "No te voy a detener." Papà drank, brought a fissured bottle to his lips like I had just told him I liked Saturdays more than Sundays. The gray of his beard went wet and he did not speak. There was no interest in him. Not an itch of care or the showing of a heart.

I did not cry, but I really felt like it.

Two days later I moved into a small contemporary home in the hills. Lucy chose the place, and since I spent hardly any time there I refused to decorate. I planned to stay only six months, but those months turned into a year, and suddenly I was going on a year and a half living in the dullest Hollywood home there was without seeing Benji much and without meeting Hal.

I was acting most of the time, attending auditions and taking on small roles where I was asked to dye my hair sun-milked oranges and blondes. I was not a celebrity but I was well-known and wanted to keep it that way. To be on a payroll as an actress but still sit in huddled waiting rooms. It was a middle ground.

As the days on-set went by, I met many celebrities; people who I thought would inspire me, push me to strive for awards and nominations, but instead they became the reason I skipped the industry's social events. They were worse than the lower class, paid far more attention to outer appearances than anybody else seemed to. Half of their days went spent beneath the hands of a doctor, skin tugged away and molded, pinched with needles by a hand of greed.

There were other actors, almost always men, who invited me out. But I declined in knowing their company would taint my image.

To be seen with one man is to also be seen as easy. To be seen as a whore. I avoided them even more as I heard the cries of other actresses, the half-spoken sentences that were never given justice, only ever blame.

I lurked on the sets with a foolish smile so other actresses might speak to me. I kept myself from saying hello first because I had learned they preferred to approach first, it made them feel dominant, and I understood that. We women hardly ever got to feel such.

The men came to me solely on the days when I painted my lashes as I had in school, or if I wore a shirt that hung low on my breasts. If I did not do this—forgot the gloss of my lips or the pluck of my brows, the directors waved me off with a curt whip of the wrist or a single word for dismissal. Nobody met my eye and I would never feel less accepted than then. I quickly learned that what I said or did here meant nothing if I was not beautiful. It was dismaying—to have done everything for beauty, just to be met with more expectations, more standards, and all I have gotten from it is empty attention and satisfaction.

My impatience grew until it was December and I was in Meghalaya India for *Beyond Summer*. The air was different, I noticed this first.

The other actors fanned themselves with a lame hand and moaned their irritations. The grounds were tucked away and swarmed by the gleaming green of grass. We walked and never met roads. They filmed and I basked in the sun and said my lines like I never had before. No wind came, and there was a thickness in the air that left our bodies sticky and slathered in sap-like sweat. But I do not remember my face resting from its smile.

I stayed three days for one scene, and when I got home, my sudden patience had not come home with me.

There was no passion in me—for any of it. The acting or the beauty or the fame. I longed to be back in India beneath the trees that had branches like tears, dripping to the grounds like the helping hand I longed to grasp. The air that had been passed through the breath and skin of sun. A place where life was not so rushed and lived for money, only.

I was already in bed, the blankets heavy around my neck and above my toes bringing warmth, but I noticed my fingers had a slight tremble to them and my lungs ached as if the room's windows had not been pried.

I left, threw on a robe and slippers, took a journal under an arm, and went onto the roof. The night was merciful, the wind not yet blowing. I breathed and breathed until my mind slowed in its pace. I wrote about impatience, faltering hope, and my exigent distaste for the life I had made for myself. I wrote and wrote till I wept, searching endlessly for reasons and answers.

I realized in minutes that I had yet to come across Hal because I was frustrated about it. All this time it was a nagging, dominating thought filling my mind.

We had walked the same halls, made deals with the same directors, both agented by the same woman, and still had yet to meet. Each time we could have, though, I felt the frustration spright in my flesh.

I should not have.

I let this be realized and finally felt solace. I would meet him at some point. It would happen, one way or another. So why not act as if it already did? Gush to Benji on the phone—talk to the neighbors—anybody who would listen—and tell them I had met Hal Moulin. Feel the pride, the overwhelming excitement. I would smile to myself in the mornings and nights and think of the first interaction we ever had. I would remember that he wore a suit when it happened. I would even recall the size of the buttons, their round and nimble shape, and I would feel that enduring all that wait was worth it. It would be far more than I had imagined, because he would know of me *before* we even met. Everything would have finally paid off, everything would be worth it, because I met Hal. I would go out dressed in outfits that would only ever be worn to meet Hal in. Every phone call I got, I would expect it to be Hal on the other line.

By the next week, Lucy calls and says I've been invited to the Academy of Television Arts award show. A day later, Hal Moulin is nominated for an Emmy.

★⁺₊★ ☾ ★⁺₊★

Over the next few weeks everything in my life is distant.

I am there, but I am not. I am buying myself a pair of vintage pointed boots, my arm moving forward, my hands cupping a wad of cash. I watch as if it is not my body, but somebody else's. I see the sum of money lying there over marble. I see how easily it is given away, because there is so much more where it comes from.

The girl takes the cash, wraps the boots in rose-colored silk. I go home and rest. I cook a small portion of pinkened salmon for dinner and go for a walk. I play a song, smooth and bleak, with 528 Hertz. I read articles on the brain's ability to discern the discrepancies between reality and imagination. I nod as if somebody has just said these things aloud. I read next that if I were to simply imagine having intimacy with another, my brain would release oxytocin, even though the intimacy never actually happened. I think of the ways I will teach this to Benji. I will tell him in the way of an old tale, but at his age now it is harder to have him hear me. It will be easier once I say the names of chemicals and hormones, the diligent pathways of neurons. When I get to bed, I am prudent and kind with my thoughts, and then I sleep.

Those weeks, I see myself from afar and realize I had become what I always wanted to be: a match for Hal Moulin.

CHAPTER THREE

"Look here!"

"Perfect!"

"Over here!"

Preston Heels walks by, a journalist on her left and a videographer on her right. Farrah Kate is posing, arms slung strategically over her shoulders, the subtle curve of her lips for a smile. Deon Blame is posing too, along with Lorena Pascal, Daya Holland, and Joss. These are the most famous actresses of our time.

I am trying to smile.

"Over here! Great, great!"

I am reminding myself to breathe.

"Look here!"

"Lorena! Look here!"

It is everything I thought—but amplified. Louder, fuller. More cameras than people, yet all I can hear are voices. Fervent, desperate voices. Mics shoved at throats, lips readily pursed.

I am trying not to squint, and trying not to make my face wide in its smile. I brush my fingers against my lips and glance down at their cherry stain, being sure there was color there still and I hadn't bitten it all away.

"Hal—Hal Moulin!"

"Mr. Moulin!"

I turn, gasp—"Hal." But the entire world chants his name now.

There is a ripple, a collective movement as everybody shifts to see him.

He is not far.

He is lean, even more so than I imagined, and bright in the flesh, walking slowly with his hands in the deep of his pockets.

"Hal!"

"Hal Moulin, over here!"

I look away, as if caught.

His name is called. Over and over and over. But Hal does not move. He stays in his place, jaw tilting up the slightest. When he speaks, finally, I know he is not far, because I can hear his voice. It is soft.

I do not move either, and I am foolish for it, standing around like the photographers, gawking and screaming internally.

Hal moves down the carpet, moving closer so he will reach the end where he will sit and accept awards with a blasé nod of his head.

I keep my palms clasped at my sides and look around once, wondering if everybody else is seeing what I am seeing, and I realize quickly that yes, we are *all* fools for Hal. Nobody can be spared.

"Hal, you're perfect!"

"Hal!"

The entire crowd is in a trance, and I am in the midst of it. I watch as they blink wildly at one another. They are different—not like my family or neighbors. They are the people I have fought to avoid. The people that smell of addiction and look like perfection. Their eyes hop from other celebrity to other celebrity, yet they all seem to linger on Hal.

"You look great, Hal."

"Prisha Sule!"

"Unreal!"

"Prisha!"

I turn. More cameras. More flashes. I remind myself to smile. I remind myself to speak. I remind myself to look at things other than Hal. The people here may be shallow, but they are not dumb.

"Prisha, you starred in *The Bluest Moon*. How was it working with Raylin West?"

"Magnificent," I stray my eyes from Hal's back. "Raylin makes my job easier than it should be."

"Did you see *The Bluest Moon* in theaters already?"

I narrow my eyes so maybe I would be able to see the interviewer better, but the cameras go where Hal goes, and he is close.

"Yes…I did. Yes."

"Did it come out the way you expected?"

"Oh, even better," I say. "Dan did an incredible job, he's an amazing director. Really."

"He is, he's amazing. So, where are you from, Prisha? I can hear that you have an accent. Did you grow up in America—or somewhere else?"

"I grew up here," I remind myself, again, to smile. "In America."

"What area, Prisha? Were you born and raised in Hollywood?"

"Here?"

"Yes. Did you grow up in Hollywood?"

The question hangs limp between us. For seconds more, I do not move or make an expression. I am not from Hollywood, but a place of poverty. A withering town. The crowd *ahhh*s behind us but I do not look away yet. I cannot admit to being born in a place like East Rey…I could shrug and grin and give no recognition to the place I was bred. I could say "yes, Hollywood" and nobody would deny me. My parents would not care, they would not even hear of it. They had no television or money to pay the telephone bill.

"No, actually…" I could lie. "I'm from—" *Rey. I'm from East Rey.* But everybody will frown, turn their heads and lips and say, *poor girl. You are not one of us.*

"I live in Hollywood now, but I grew up on the Eastside of Rey," I flash my teeth, because Prisha-in-my-mind does not know insecurity. "East Rey is…I came from a very low-income area so being here…is a…it is a shock."

"Wow," The interviewer nods and nods. Every action here must be exaggerated, but this one does not seem so forced. "I'm sure that is a shock! All the way from East Rey. Your town must be so proud of their wunderkind."

"Over here!"

"So how did you end up *here*, Prisha?"

"Prisha?"

From the corner of my eye, there is a looming figure, and flashes of light coming with it. A gander of hair, curly at its tips. Bones high on their cheeks. Every ounce of my being is conscious of his own. I feel my back straighten, my legs shake, my smile become its most brilliant.

"Prisha? How did you do it? How did you get from rags to riches?"

"Manifestation."

"Sorry?"

I lick my lips and try to rid the stringent feel of them. "I practice intentional manifestation and divination."

It is not something Prisha-in-my-mind would have admitted, but Hal is standing nearby and if he would not look at me—this was all for nothing. The fame, the beauty, the speeches. It was all for a simple word or beckon. Without it, every effort I ever made was all for nothing.

"*Divination?* As in, black magic? The Devil's work?"

"Oh, no. I think…I think that's maybe just a biblical belief. They created the idea of the Devil, I believe. What I mean is…I'm using the power of faith to my advantage."

"Faith? What sorts of things do you do, then? How did divination get you here, today?"

"Well…I can make things happen easily. With my will. With my words or thoughts. I learned…I learned about three years ago and I went from living in poverty with no career to being…here."

"Wow. So you're here tonight because of divination? Because of the spells you have cast?"

"Well, sure. Yes. The fame—my attendance tonight. Yeah."

"Wow. That sounds like magic. Is it magic, Prisha? Would you call yourself a witch, Prisha Sule?"

I see her bend forward, the sudden intrigue in the gape of her lips. I realize that she has made sure to use my name in this sentence. It will be written. Recorded.

"Well, I wouldn't call myself—"

"A witch?"

"Who's a witch?"

Heads turn, their faces all stricken and damp as they smile at the interviewer and I. For a second, I think maybe she will change topics because more famed people have shown interest. But she does not.

"It sounds like that to me."

"No—not really. I think anybody who just—"

"Who's a witch?"

"Who can cast spells? Can you do one for me?"

There is laughter and more dampness. Bodies inch forward, as if they have heard the word that lures. *Witch*, I have learned, is what you make of it.

The next morning, the paper is printed. Nobody wrote about *The Hope Game* or *The Bluest Moon*. Nobody printed Hal's picture, or Daya Holland's. Or perhaps they did, but nobody bought it. Every reporter's headline read, *The Witch of Hollywood,* and below was a timeless sort of beauty wearing a bell-sleeved gown and sleek dotted white eyeliner. Behind me is a boy, his eyes widened the slightest bit.

It was the first time Hal Moulin had ever looked at me when I wasn't already looking first.

CHAPTER FOUR

I wake to the scent of herbs. Sage. Clouds and clusters of it.

I am not in my Hollywood house—I am home. The blinds are drawn with one panel tied tightly to another so the light will not be let in.

For hours, I do not get up. I do not move, really, but when I do, it is to gag out the remains of what I ate the day before.

There is a bucket beside me, a damp towel, and a mug of water.

"Prisha." *Pree-shah.* The way my mother says my name. The way it was meant to be said.

"Prisha."

More Sage.

"¿Qué hiciste?"

I do not remember at first.

Smoke brushes the hot of my face, making me more red and more flushed and feeling as if I have an herb to my mouth. Then it comes to me. Flooding my aching, battered mind.

I sit up and remember Hal. His tallness. His mundane way of being. The Interview. The questions. Divination. Anxiety. Benji.

In my feigned sleep I had heard Mom speak. Her voice a rush of bind, telling Papà I would be staying for the night, because of Benji. Benji had been at a schoolmate's house watching the television. He saw me on screen, the word "witch" for a caption. When I heard this, all that seemed to matter was the fact that Benji cared about who I was now. I did not dwell on the photographs or my sour mouth or the fact that Benji had friends with enough means for a television at home. He was keeping track of me even though my parents forbade it.

"Prisha, get up."

"A man is at the door. Está preguntando por ti."

I pry my eyes and see her standing at the edge of the sofa, angry, with no idea of my successes. Or perhaps she does, hence the Sage cleanse—and Benji, and it all means nothing to her.

"Prisha, get up."

It is the first time I have seen her in months. She is the same, but angrier. More lines and creases. I cannot help but feel this was my doing. Even though I have tried to help, sent envelopes with money and letters of plea asking them to move into my new home. Just one word of acceptance and I would be there to bring them, I said. And if not them, then at least Benji, I said. But my family would not hear it. The envelopes appeared back in my mailbox, the letters unreplied to. I understood this, though I wished I had not, but in our culture, loyalty is above all. Over the years, pride has come to amount the same.

"Prisha."

"Trata con ese hombre para que se vaya."

"Who? What man?"

I rise, run my fingers through my hair, and stumble till my palm meets the knob.

"Tu bufanda! Ponte tu bufanda. ¿Qué estás haciendo?"

Bile rises in my throat again and I wrap my scarf around my head so that only my eyes will be shown. She does not know that I am allowed to walk without it. How does she not know?

My palm grasps the knob and my body's weight is leaned upon it. At the door is a man. Quent Brose, one of Hal's bodyguards. He is much older, with a startlingly youthful face. He has Papà's same shade of brown skin and graying hair.

"Prisha Sule?"

"Yes…morning. Goodmorning."

"Goodmorning. I've come to request your presence at the Moulin residence. Hal would like to speak with you, ma'am. He'd like you to come over for a chat."

For seconds, I cannot speak.

"…Sorry?"

"Hal Moulin. He would like to meet with you."

"Hal?"

"Yes. I believe you might have seen him last night at the award ceremony. He was there."

I nod to show that I agree, but Quent knows as well as I do that I have known of Hal since long before yesterday.

"When are you available to come and chat, miss?"

"Um, well…"

"He's available at ten am, three pm, and seven pm. Today."

If I was any bit pale, I might have blanched. "Today?"

"Yes."

"To…talk? With Hal?"

"Yes."

I have questions, too many, but I would be a fool to pry and lose this.

"Seven," I say. "Seven works for me."

By 3pm, I am back in Hollywood. But before I left, I knelt at my parents' side and thanked them. Papà looked away, at Benji, and I knew it was his wordless way of telling me to thank him instead. I ruffled Benji's hair, pressed my lips to his forehead. Thanked and thanked till he grinned and said, "Why're you still here? Isn't *Hal Moulin* waiting for you?"

Another kiss and I left.

By 4pm my hair is dyed red, then black, and left in a sultry shade of burgundy. Antoni does my makeup and chooses what silk to drape across my body. I am wealthy enough to wear what I please but Quent had asked one thing of me, and it was to wear a scarf.

By 5pm, I vomit. I decide I am sick.

"I think maybe I should just let…let them know that I won't be able to make it after all. I was sick all night, anyway. So it would just make sense that I rest…Oh God, I think I'll have to."

Antoni looks at me.

"You're right," I say, although he has not replied. "But no, really. I really do feel awful."

"Really?" He says. "You're going to Hal Moulin's *house*," and that is all. Antoni is my usual stage artist. We do not know each other well. We've given each other coffees and compliments but never more, and even he knows what it means for me to be invited somewhere by Hal Moulin.

"You're right."

By 7pm, I am there. The front door is pulled open, and then there is Hal. I see him before I see the rest.

"He'll speak with you in just a moment,"

I nod.

Nod, nod, nod. And watch.

He moves across the room, and I think he will be suddenly sequestered away. Pulled into another room where I will never get my chance. But then he is suddenly closer. And closer. Avid in speech. Different when the cameras are not around. Standing taller, nodding to show that he is really listening. That is when I notice, there are five other girls in the room. All five feet and seven inches tall, the same as I, wrapped in their scarves, only the brown of their eyes showing. I would ask what they're doing here, so that maybe I will know what *I'm* doing here, but I cannot speak. I cannot squeal or cry or laugh, I can only smile.

I am smiling.

"—for making it here today. I appreciate it," He tells one.

I move even closer, my feet shuffling in their walk. Everything I have ever imagined I would say to him vanishes, and I am left with a happiness so strong I feel faint. *Hal is here. I am in Hal's house.* My skin seems to buzz and tremble, my heart loud in its living.

"Hello—" I hear him say, his voice careful in the way of a whisper. Calm in the ways we are not.

"—nice to meet you."

Their hands extend and shake. I can see now his hair is curlier up-close, whirling across in careful loops as if placed there by hand. Skin bright, without flaw, with subtle markings of hair above his lip and chin that I could never make out before.

I blink and blink.

"Ah—hi," Hal turns, the movement is rapid and graceful, but still I am startled. "Your name?"

"Prisha Sule." I clasp my hands together, tight, so he will not see their tremble.

But you can call me Pris. Or Pree. Or Prisha.

But my voice does not come. Not a breath.

"Will Sule do? I'm referring to you all by last name."

"Yes. Sule is fine."

"Alright."

I think he expects me to speak next, but all I can think is, *you're real.* He nods again. *You're real, you're real, you're real.*

"Alright," Hal turns his back to me. "Everybody make line, please."

"Me, too?"

"Yes," He says, not even turning to look at me when he says it. "You too."

I get in line with my cheeks blotchy like a caught child, my fingers clasped in their shame.

He had looked me in the eye, but barely. *I've ruined it.*

It was too fast—the way he left my side to stand at the front of the room. Too fast.

I watch as he looks around, perusing the others with his head moving up and down knowingly.

He looks at the other girls he had conversations with. The ones who actually *spoke* about something other than their names. His eyes linger on one. My mouth opens, closes. My heart goes starved, skipping its beats.

"You," Hal points. "You can leave."

The girl beside me nods, obeys.

"You too. Leave…"

There is an exhale, a sharp outtake of breath.

"Thank you…"

"And you, to her right."

He's going to kick me out, I know it, and I don't even know what the fuck I'm in line for. The nerves I once had go stale, smoothly replaced by dread. By sadness. Humiliation. *Of course, of course, of course.* So easily, I am miserable.

"And you, to her right."

And then his head tilts ever so slightly, eyes meeting mine. For those seconds, I have died and come alive again.

"It must be Sule then," He says, eyes low. "I knew it quickly, so that must mean you are The Witch. Yes?"

He brings his hand up and flicks it, uttering a word of gratitude beneath his breath, and the last girl leaves at once.

" —asked you here because, well, according to—"

There is a sharp clicking sound and the door is pushed open. A short blonde enters, she is lovely and solemn looking. Hal does not acknowledge her, and so it is a shock even to me that I can tell he likes her.

"Hi," she says.

Hal goes on, not replying, but his shoulders and chest seem to broaden. It is enough for me to know.

"From what I read and heard last night, anything I want you can bring into fruition. This is…this is correct?"

She is wearing all gray. Pants oversized and drifting off of a jutting hip bone. If she were to jump, I suspect they would fall from her body and sag to the ground.

I turn back to Hal and blink, as if I am seeing him for the first time. Noticing the dark of his hair and the level of his eyes. Hearing the indifferent way of his voice and the slimness of his nostrils.

He is looking at me, nodding as he speaks, and his left hand begins to unfurl. Left open as if it awaits another.

"I want you to work for me," He says, and the blonde slips her hand into his. There is a buzz, a shimmer of energy between them. Something only lovers obtain. I have seen it many times, and have never been wrong in my estimations.

I stare. That is all I can do.

Hal shifts to make a face at the blonde and she grins.

I nod, numbly. "Work?" I ask, with no spring of excitement. No care. No thoughts of what is to come or the hopes I might have for it. I can only think of what I am seeing and feeling now.

Confusion. Desperation and anger.

"Yeah. I'm not entirely sure yet what you're cap…"

He might have said something else, something important, but my mind speaks over all else. *You are in love already*, I think. I think it over and over.

In my mind, I am sticking my finger in the air and pressing it to the flat of his chest. I am telling him why I am here, and all I have done to do so. How I have made myself look this way, for him. All so that he would like me. How I have become polished and feminine and without a physical flaw and yet, he would not have chosen me.

"Would you…be interested?"

"In what…interested in what?"

"In working for me. With me. Helping me, I mean."

"Why would I help you?"

It takes the skip of my pulse to realize I have spoken aloud.

"Well…" He says. "Why wouldn't you?"

…and then I see the blonde scowling, at me. And I'm angry again.

"Because you're selfish," I say, and gape for it.

I do not even have the dignity to apologize, I simply stand with my fingers pressed to my mouth. Hal does not speak, his head turning slowly, as if he is curious.

Curious, not insulted.

He's *curious*. And I will take that from him.

"…because you already have everything. What would you need help for? There are so many people…the people…Most of them are suffering mental health issues and lack of finances…and you have everything, you're a celebrity, the most famous one, and yet you want me to work for *you* so that *you* can have more?"

"It is—it is the most selfish thing I have heard."

For moments, there is only the sound of my breathing, heavy and swift.

Hal beckons his head as if he would agree, "Yes…you're right." But there is no emotion there. "You're right."

"Is she?" The blonde says.

Hal crosses his arms over his chest, leaving her hands on their own. She wishes to speak again, to say more. I can see it in the blue of her eyes.

"She is, but still," He nods. "My request stands. And I will pay you for your help."

My back straightens to match his own. "But—why should I accept? The money is—it is hardly an incentive for me."

"You're not interested in the money?"

"No."

"Really?" He asks flatly. "You're an actress, though."

"Yes, but I'm not in this business for the money."

"Well then, I will give you anything you want, if the pay isn't what you want. Anything can be yours, just name it."

The blonde laughs and says, "She can already have anything she wants, though. She's a *witch.*"

I do not look at her—I fear that it would bring satisfaction. So my eyes remain on Hal. And I begin to feel rude, disgraceful, and childish even, but still, I cannot bring myself to give her attention. I take in his white long sleeve, his black slacks. *What had I missed? What led me so astray? Why did I think looking this way would—*

"Sule?" He calls, and despite my anger, my face flushes again. "*Is* there anything I can possibly grant you?"

"I don't know."

"Anything at all?"

"I'm not…sure."

"Just name it."

"I'm going to think about it," I am backing away as I say this. I am thinking that this cannot be real. That this is not what I planned…but what had I expected? That I would meet Hal and it'd be love at first sight? That Hal Moulin would be single his entire life? That he wouldn't fall in love until he met *me*?

"I'm going to think about it."

By 3pm the next day, Hal Moulin receives a letter.

Five words, all lowercase.

one condition, we work alone

CHAPTER FIVE

For hours his face replays in my mind. I am in the kitchen, the hall, the patio, and I see the lift of his brow. The quick movement of his lips. I see the nod of his head and hear the ease of his laughter. I feel afire, a match brought to wax, as if it is happening all over again. His eyes on mine. Him speaking. To me.

It is only a fever dream now. Hal, but better. Polite and humorous and calm, while I had been bashful and rude and skittish. There should be no excuses, but I make them; I had prepared myself for stardom and attention, questions and rumors and even the downfall of my independence, but not for the prospect that Hal would *not* be mine. Worse, that he was already somebody else's. And she is nothing like me, the blonde.

Stylish and bred of nepotism. One mother a famous American model and the other mother an old-time actress.

She is beautiful in a modern way, and gamine but not shamed for it because of her size and color.

I take my journal and write. About regrets and humiliation. About obsession and disbelief, severe adoration, and my one condition.

It is only two days later when the mail comes. I rush to my drawers, patt blush on my cheeks and stain my lips red.

The letter's edges are shriveled by fire for the effect of parchment, the ink-like oil not yet smeared. They ask for my discretion and a signature of agreement.

A day later, another letter comes. It is different. The paper is lined, taken from a notebook, and creased at its corners. I hold it, refuse to let it part from my hands. *Hal*, it says. Signed by Hal. The letters are all plain and sleek. Casual. I read it twice, then seven times, twenty, maybe more, before I realize what it says.

I am not sure what my face becomes, but I am sure it is foolish.

Three days pass, and I show up in all red. Dark, burgundy, red. My collar bones jut and brag from above the fabric, the sleeves drip from my wrists in their bell-sleeved shape. I am trying, mostly, not to think. To just show up, smile, and act as if we are friends. As if we have been all this time.

When the door opens, I realize two things. One, that I have intentionally manifested this, and two, I should have taken some fucking notes.

CHAPTER SIX

"Should I...do you need..."

The room has been emptied of people. Hal has stuck to his word; there is no sight of the blonde. It is only him and I, and he is looking at me.

I shake my head, feeling bare and panicked and blessed.

"Only you," I say. But it is too late, Hal is uncovering the stout altar beside us. With the silk cast away, I can see the crystals, sage, and oils. There are vials already filled to their caps with dried rose petals and wispy feathers. "Just you..."

He shrugs suggestively. "You don't need any of this?"

"No," I say, and smile. Apparently I am never not smiling. The pink in my cheeks is a stain. The grin, a permanent bend of my lips.

"Unless…a method of mine is the placebo effect. So if you would like to make use of the crystals, then by all means…"

"No, no. Whatever you think," He shrugs again and takes the seat across from mine. "I know nothing. Of the placebo…of crystals."

"Okay…well," I stand with my hands behind my back. "I'm really sorry. About everything I said. The other day."

"It's fine," Hal turns his head. He is curious again. "Don't worry about it. I understand, we all have our…off days."

He must take my silence for embarrassment, because he says, "You're a lot nicer today, that's how I know it was an off day."

I laugh, but I am ashamed. "I was rude. And caught off guard. I don't think you're selfish. At all. I think you're brilliant."

"Brilliant," he repeats, and he is no longer so curious. He is doubtful. "I'm not the one who can make things happen with my mind."

"You can, though," I say. "And I will prove it to you."

He smiles almost, beckons his head, "Alright, then."

"So, do you—do you know what you want? I mean, can you give me an example of what it is you want?"

"Anything? Big? Minor?"

"Anything you can think of."

"Sure, alright." He nods, his fingers intertwined. I think for a second that he is nervous, but Hal Moulin does not get nervous. "I want an Oscar."

I open my mouth to speak, I almost say that he does not need a witch for that, but he says something else.

"I'm not—I'm just not sure that I'll win. But I want to."

"You…you don't think you'll win?"

"Well…the others, the new coming actors, they have advantages I did not. They're starting their careers earlier and taking improvisation classes than I never got the chance to take." He says this as if it is fact; their success set in stone. "And they're younger. That's always a bad thing. The younger the better, and…"

I feel my smile falter, my cheeks drop. They are not as talented as you, I think. They are not as anything as you. But I do not say it.

"Okay, then. The first thing we will work on is altering the thoughts of your conscious mind, then we will work on changing your subconscious, too. It's easier that way, instead of going straight to some kind of hypnosis."

"Altering them?"

"Um, yes. We have to change the thoughts you're having."

He bobs his head. "Ok, alright. May I—may I ask a question?"

I nod, once again stunned by his boyish manners. "Yes. Of course. Of course you may."

"Okay, why do we need to change my mind, exactly?"

"Because," I clear my throat, trying to sound simple. "Because you can only have what you believe you can have."

★⁺₊★ ☾ ★⁺₊★

"Wait," Dustin curses herself for interrupting, but she must know. "He was perfect?"

"He..."

"I mean, he sounds perfect."

Prisha shrugs. "I think I just make him seem that way."

She says this more to herself than to Dustin, "But he was perfect. To me."

"To me, too, I think."

"Well, if I was not so mad about him—I'd say he was better in some ways, and not, in others."

"In what ways? Why not?"

"Hal was like many other people in the industry—or in the world, for that matter."

"Oh," Dustin nods, as if she might already know what is to come. Quickly, she regrets having asked. "I think I know what you mean."

"Yes, he was not an exception to the lifestyle—there, in Hollywood. He slept with many people. Men and women. And…as much as the jealousy sickened me, I didn't care enough to leave. And I can't even bring myself to feel shame for it—even now—that I decided to wait."

"I did not want to be just another person he slept with, of course, I wanted him to know me. First, at least. And I was willing to wait."

"Did he? Did he ever truly get to know you?"

"Yes, I think. He saw me, finally. But, it was late."

"Late?"

"It was too late."

The next time I see Hal, it is at the Bublé film festival. He is wearing a velvet suit, blue and bright. People have bunched in small cliques, clinging to the industry's freshest. Most of them are at Hal's side. He nods and nods, listens more than speaks.

I am making my way toward the actress Pennela Lopez when an older woman known as Bebe takes hold of my arm.

"Prisha Sule?"

"Ah, hello Bebe." I feel odd calling her this; An older woman, "baby". Benji might have laughed hearing it.

"You're a pretty thing," She says. She is draped in white. Patches of white, all different tones. Cream, ivory, pearl. She starred in *Seventies Best* when I was five years old and her career spiked from then on, all the way through this year's remake of *Dune Tribune.* "Even more beautiful in real life."

"Oh, my, thank you," I say, and try not to make my face so wide while I smile. "So are you. It's so nice to meet you."

We hold each other's arms, this is how most women here greet one another.

"It's nice to meet you as well. You know, I read The Central's paper," Her lips press, dampening. "It's the biggest thing this week."

"Right, yes. The Central," I shrug, making myself innocent. "That was my first and *last* recorded interview."

"Really?"

"Yes," I laugh and cluck my tongue. "I think so."

"But all that publicity, darling, it'll get you somewhere."

I had agreed and smiled, but I had not lied about turning down future interviews. Years later, I would be known for my secrecy.

"Back when I was your age, before The Central was popular, it was The Teacup. They printed 3 million issues of *Selling Souls For Fame.* Did you ever read that paper?"

"No, I don't think I did."

Bebe wiped her forehead with a satin sleeve and said, "The entire article was about me, Bebe Reid, age 16, maybe 17. I told an interviewer about my upbringing. I wasn't religious, but I practiced spirituality—which was a huge part of my raising. My mother always told me that I was the creator of my life, not some man in the sky from a book called 'Bible'. And I told the interviewer that, thinking it was inspiring, right? It was. To me, it still is. I didn't even mention Jesus—all I said was that I am the creator, but I was called a Witch."

"Ah, like me."

"Yes. Except, back then, it had no good connotation. And even now it has its moments, but since you're beautiful, it is different. Back then…back then people were putting up posters that said I should be burned at the stake. Said I was an evil spirit. Somebody who worked with the Devil."

I realize I have been shaking my head. I stop moving.

"I replied in another interview, out of desperation, and said I'd never believed in witchcraft. My point is, there is no difference between what you and I did. Same practices, same law. The people of America are the same as twenty, thirty, forty, years ago. But since you fit today's beauty standards, you are praised for being a witch. I still get hell for it, and teenagers today idolize you."

"I…I know," I smile in my discomfort. "And I only look this way because I knew it would get me here. The reputation that I have…I knew."

Bebe nods. "So, then, tell me, out of everything you can manifest, why fame?"

I almost tell her that fame, now, seems useless.

I have long been aware of the materialism and shallowness, and still, I stand in the same expensive silks and faux furs, supporting the rich and privileged. *Being* the rich and privileged. I am one of them.

"Because it's a stepping stool," I say this frantically, as if I must prove myself before she is gone and will not hear my excuses. "It's just something I needed on the path to what I actually want."

"Ah," Bebe's eyes flicker behind me. "I see."

"When I get it, though, what I want, I'll be done with this industry. But…thank you. For reminding me…of our reality—"

"Don't thank me, honey. I only told you this so you would understand a different aspect, but it seems you already know. So it is not so different. But please," She pats my arm. "You have no reason to thank me."

"Hello, Bebe. Sule, hello."

My eyes flash open.

"Ah, darling Hal. How is the night treating you?"

Beside me, Hal beckons his head ever so slightly to hear Bebe speak. His lips are tilted upward in a half-smile. I find my lips doing the exact opposite, tilting down.

"It's going fine. The movie trailers should be starting soon, I think."

"Yes, I sure hope so," She takes his arm. She is holding us both now. "I'm getting tired, I really do need to take a seat."

"Oh, should I—" Hal does not even finish, he is off and searching for a chair and returns in seconds, setting the piece of furniture right there in the middle of the room. Bebe laughs, as if Hal has done this once or twice before.

"Oh, Hal—" He is back, his smile the same, as if he does not deserve praise. "—thank you. No man could compare," Yes. *I know.* Bebe takes the seat, settling her hands over her lap. She is still smiling when she looks up at me—and freezes.

"Dear girl, what is it? Are you alright? You look like you've just seen a ghost."

Fuck.

"Oh, no—everything's fine. All good."

"Are you sure?"

"Yes! Of course. It was—really, very sweet of you—Hal, to bring Bebe a chair." I blink. Blink, blink, blink.

Bebe looks from me to Hal, from Hal to me, and a new kind of smile settles. *Fuck.*

"It was no trouble," Hal says. He is looking at Bebe as he speaks. As am I. "None at all."

"How did you two meet?" Bebe asks, her finger teasing the air between us.

Hal does not say, his head tilts from side to side, as if he is thinking of an answer. "I think—"

"Oh. At the Emmys," I say. "I believe."

"Yes," Hal agrees. "Well, I think the day after."

Bebe makes a sound, nodding, and returns to her impish smile.

Hal nods back. "Well then, I'll see you both when the awards begin. Be sure to bid me goodbye before you take off, alright Bebe? Or—will I see you at Anderson's afterward?"

"Lore Anderson's?"

"Yes."

"Oh, no. I don't think I will, that's not my crowd anymore."

I listen silently, turning my head and nodding when appropriate. I had heard of Anderson's parties before, rumored and compared to the tale of Gatsby's.

"Are you sure? I can have Quent drive you home whenever you'd like."

"No, no, it's all right, thank you, Hal. But best of luck at the Academy Awards, dearest boy. I have no doubts about you."

"Thank you." Hal nods at her, then at me. But I'm still staring straight down at Bebe. Even after he leaves, she is smirking.

"Dear girl, you don't need fame for *that*. *I* can be your stepping stool."

I do not say anything for a few seconds. I breathe out.

"You just were."

Bebe and I exchanged phone numbers and by the time the clock reaches eleven-thirty, I am tipsy. My third glass of wine had been emptied briskly and the world became a bit sweeter, the people a bit funnier. Even as I am speaking with the other actresses, I am thinking of how I am really no match for Hal. Even with the most beauty and kindness and intelligence, nobody is like Hal. I was rude and unforgivable the first time we met—just the other day—and he acts as if I have done nothing. As if I deserve respect as well as anybody else. I excuse myself and walk over to a new platter of bright wine as a woman spins around. Right then, I am thinking of Hal bringing Bebe a seat, Hal nodding politely. My stomach churns with a pain I have not felt before—it is odd, like a painless sting. The woman places her arms before her chest, shielding herself, and in turn pushes the glass to me, and in half a second, wine is dripping down both our chests.

"Oh, Lord have mercy." Her eyes go wide and petrified, the green in them spirited. Her tube top is velvet, smushed and soaked at its edges. Hal remembering where we first met. Hal correcting me.

"Oh no. Oh gosh."

I am about to tell her that it's fine, really, I didn't pay for the dress anyway, when she scream-whispers, "You're *gorgeous*."

"Oh. Thank you, so are you."

She has dark hair and skin, black eyeliner, a black lip ring, chains around her neck, and boots. But she herself is light mannered, soft-spoken and moving in a strategized grace.

"I...I ruined your dress." She blinks at me, eyes trailing down my chest.

"Oh, it's just a stain."

"I'm so sorry."

"It's okay. Really," I wave my hand dismissively. "The dress is so dark you can't even see the wine."

"But—but it must reek."

I bend my face forward. She is right, we do reek.

"It's okay," I wave my hand again. "It's okay. It's fine. Actually, this gives me an excuse to leave early, so I should be thanking you. Thanks."

The girl shifts to put her body's weight on the other leg. "Oh, now I feel just horrible. You shouldn't—if you leave early because of this—look, somebody can get it out. There are workers with supplies in the—" She's nodding her head, gesturing toward the double doors nearby. "—if I can just get my hands on—"

"No, really, it's alright."

"It's not. That dress must have been—"

"What's your name?"

"Aimee. It's Aimee."

"I'm Prisha."

"I know."

She is staring at me in a way I have not been stared at before. Her lips part slowly, long lashes fluttering. I do not say it, but she reminds me of the character Bambi.

"You do?"

"Yes," She says. "You know Hal Moulin."

Aimee leans forward, as if the movement is accidental, but I can tell it is not. She has spoken with conviction, so much that I begin to cough, my throat suddenly sour in its taste.

"Right?"

"Yes. I have met him," I say. "Once or twice."

She nods, "Yeah." She is no longer Bambi, no longer so innocent-looking. "Three times, now."

"How…"

"He doesn't date other actors, you know."

I feel my body go rigid. "What?"

"So don't get your hopes up," She then turns and adjusts the bobby pins on her head. I stare after her, wondering how long she has known of me, and what I did wrong, but the answer is simple. She is after Hal, and so I say one last thing. I move forward, only a swift step.

"Threats are only provoked by other threats."

She spins around, lips parted, but I am already walking away.

Years later, I would think back to that night and remember Aimee before Hal, just for a fleeting second.

★⁺₊★ ☾ ★⁺₊★

Vivian Astora does not enjoy award shows, press release parties, or film festivals. She likes to wear dresses and slacks, but only if nobody is looking. Makeup and public speaking is endurable, but she's had enough of that for a lifetime. With two mothers and a boyfriend that all live to serve in the entertainment industry, she has accepted that Hollywood will always be in her life.

It is past midnight when Hal comes home. She waited till the Bublé film festival was over, at exactly 12:45 am, to drive to Hal's.

He is sitting outside, waiting, still dressed in the blue velvet that makes his skin look like the moon melted and leaked.

"No after-party?"

"Nope. Well yes, but I'd rather be here."

"Really?" She grins. "Don't you like those little gatherings Anderson has, though?"

"I do," Hal says, taking her coat as they walk up the steps.

"Then?"

"I don't know. Nobody there interests me. Nobody to connect with. And I just didn't feel like going."

Vivian shifts to look at Hal, the movement quick. She was foolish as a child, so easily bribed and lied to. But as an adult, she unfailingly trusts her intuition. Hal's *grand-mere* Chesca had told her to.

"I'd rather be with you," He adds.

"Alright," She says, because tonight, *tonight,* she decided to ignore it.

CHAPTER SEVEN

On Thursday Lucy calls and tells me to get on-set for *Merrier Without Mistletoe.* I pull on my stockings and throw my keys into my purse with a tube of lipstick.

It is March, but the studio wears Christmas ornaments and holds pillows with their foams spilling out for faux snow. There is coffee and no food. I am hungry and restless and jittery, but this part will pay more than just the bills.

"Prisha!" Delirah comes out from behind the curtains and beckons me, grinning.

"Hi, Delirah. Good Morning."

"Come on, come on. Come here."

I follow. I am especially polite to her; she is the lead casting director.

"This is for you," She says, fluttering her fingers at the door. "All yours."

From what everybody else can see I am patting at my cheeks, wiping away tears that never welled.

"Oh, wow. That is so…" Gold and tacky. "Wow. Thank you so much."

I clasp my hands at my chest. It is the first room I've been assigned that has a label, a plaque in the middle of the door. It reads *The Witch of Hollywood.*

"It's so beautiful."

I can see at least the charm in the label and flush by the hand of my ego.

But then I am shrinking away, wondering if anybody in America will remember my actual name.

They will hear 'witch' and be taken from their trances. They will hear 'Prisha' and go on as if there had been no interruption—but this is what I wanted. My head lifts, remembering that it would not matter if I was known. Years from now I would be free to leave and there would be no name to trace. I would be forgotten.

"Jelly, come take a photograph of Prisha in front of her dressing room."

"Stand right under it, Prisha."

"Yes, just there."

I have my hands at my hips, head tilted to the right, lips high on my cheeks. Jelly takes two or ten pictures, has me do about four different poses before he scampers back on-set. I spend about an hour and a half in the dressing room, my hair and face tugged and patted with powders while I read the script.

It is a comedy, but the lines are without amusement; they have been overplayed, and I am almost never the underdog.

"Somebody's knocking…" Antoni says.

"Oh…Yes?"

"Who is it?"

"Jessica Romero from *The Bubbly House*," The voice is giddy and sweet. "I was wondering if I could ask Prisha Sule a few questions for an interview. It'll only take about ten minutes."

Antoni shrugs, looks at me in waiting. "Your call."

"Come on in, then."

The journalist enters. She is wearing her hair in an old fashioned updo, I can see this beneath the white of her scarf.

She has an electric pen in hand, lipstick stark and red. Her eyes are attentive, her focus solely on me.

"Hi, Prisha! Hello!" Her hand pokes out for me to shake. "It's so nice to meet you in person—such an honor."

"Hi, I like the way you've done your hair," I lean forward, my hand reaching for hers, but Antoni slaps my hand away playfully—"No, no. She can't shake hands right now."

"Oof, okay. Sorry. This'll only take a few minutes."

"Sure, so long as it's not recorded."

Jessica smiles, but it becomes nervous as she points to her waist. A small blinking device is there, strapped against the curve of a hip. "You don't...you don't want it recorded?"

"No. I only do written interviews, is that alright?"

"Of course, yes," She places the device in her bag, and I am sure to smile graciously. "So, I saw you in your latest film, *The Bluest Moon*, where you play a young jewish girl who has an affair with an older woman, who happens to be the director of the summer camp."

"Right."

"I mean, it is a miracle that you aren't up there with Farrah Kate and Daya Holland yet. You did *spectacularly* on that film. The way that your eyes—your eyes alone—show how your heart breaks! Before you even see the wife, you are already so crestfallen. Can you tell me how you are able to depict experiences and emotions like that so authentically?"

"Thank you. I, um, I suppose it takes a lot of research. I watched numerous films prior to *The Bluest Moon* that entailed themes of desperation and youth interacting with people of older ages—and anguish for love."

Jessica nods. Nods, writes, nods, and writes. As if she is really, *truly* hearing me.

"Also, imagination, of course, was a huge part. Every movie requires a degree of imagination. I really just have to put myself in the character's shoes and do my best to cultivate those emotions and put them onto—onto my face, I guess," I look to my arms and remember their sudden looseness. "My whole body, really."

"Right, yes. So, are you able to retrieve any of those emotions from past experiences and bring them on-set? Do you ever think back to a time when you, yourself, were dealing with heartbreak in a relationship? Do you use that while filming?"

My arm lifts and I scratch the back of my neck. It is a gesture of diffidence. I quickly lower my hand and smile.

"Not exactly. It's mostly imagination."

"Wow. Usually actors become triggered by a scene and react from a personal perspective but that is amazing. That you can separate the two."

"Well, you see, I've only been in one relationship and it was never officially labeled, and I've never really been in love with somebody like that—the way the characters I play, have."

"Really?" Jessica leans forward, all ears and hands. "You've *never* been in love?"

I shake my head as Megan comes to mind. I hope foolishly that she stays away from newspapers and magazine gossip. Somehow, even now, I remember her austere ways of affection and fear the hurt I might have caused.

"Not once in my life, no, unless you count a celebrity," I laugh, just barely. "Then you can say I've been desperately in love."

"Wow. Well, now that you're a celebrity, surely you have a chance with them."

"I wouldn't say I'm a celebrity. Not really."

"But you're famous, for sure," She says, and Antoni nods his head in a way of agreement. "Have you met them yet? Worked with them on-set at all? Who is it that you were desperately in love with?"

I look up and see Antoni's head tilt. I shake my head once. He winces, as if he might have wanted to know my answer as well as Jessica did.

"Okay, Jessica, honey," He says. "Ten minutes are up. Sorry, but we need you to leave."

"Thank you for your questions, Jessica. It was lovely to meet you."

She is smiling so big, so happily, you would think I had given her Hal's name and address. Even at the door, she is nodding and nodding, saying thank you repeatedly. I meet the eyes of Antoni once again and see the pithy shake of his head, and know we are thinking the same damn thing.

I check the newsstands every morning for two weeks after that. The television is always on so there is a constant buzz at home, but *The Bubbly House* has only put out one article, and it is written on the trendiest scarf a lower class could wear. One with beads tinted gold and made in a shape that is meant to outline the jaw. At the very bottom, there is an Ad warning people to keep their scarves on; removal would be self-cruelty, but by the hands of an officer.

Another week, and there is no mention of a witch in Hollywood. I cannot help but think Jessica is waiting for something. But if she had my words, she needs nothing else. I decided to shrug the interview off and focus on my lines for *Merrier Without Mistletoe.* I go to a costume fitting and trim my hair an inch. A week later, Jessica Romero puts out a new article for *The Bubbly House* called, *From Desperate Fan to Desperate Lover: Prisha Sule and Aimee Vare.*

Who the fuck is Aimee Vare?

CHAPTER EIGHT

The whole time I'm reading the article, I'm saying, "I don't even know who Aimee is. I've never met an Aimee in my life."

But then I am so quickly distracted by the photograph, and it is a shame to realize how much I am disappointed with what I see. The bend of my back, the minor swell of my belly that showed the wine's rest. I wince at this till my eyes flutter back to the girl, and I do remember her. Bambi.

The wine. The black batting eyelashes. The threat. It is all there, and in the middle of the page, just below the words, *"you can say I've been desperately in love"*, is a picture of me at the Bublé film festival, looking absolutely, utterly, in love. My hands are at my chest, my fingers laced tightly, but it is my eyes that tell all. There is a figure—out of the shot—that must be Hal. But Aimee stands before him, and Aimee is staring at me.

I grab my phone and skim the letters and loitering names, determined to put this article to an end, *but there is no one to call.* When a rumor is spread, it cannot be buried or wiped clean. It can only be topped.

I breathe out, my heart a throb as the telephone begins to buzz in my cold palms.

"Lucy—"

"You read it?"

"Yes. It's my fault, I shouldn't have said all that about love and other celebrities. I know you've told me before to keep other people's names out of my mouth and I did, but obviously that wasn't enough and—"

"This isn't all a bad thing, you know."

"What? It's a lie. I talked to her—to Aimee—once. And I never—"

"Prisha, people have been wondering about your dating life since you got into this industry. It's the most asked question when it comes to your career and they finally got content regarding the matter. Trust me, it's not that bad." She repeats this, *it's not that bad.*

"It'll blow over. Ally Cadena was lesbian. Ren Love was bisexual. Their careers were fine."

I had not considered this, my own *career*.

"I worry more that they're calling me lesbian. I'm—I like both men and women, but I do not want...I do not want people to think I only like women."

"Oh, okay then."

"Yeah."

"Then you don't need to say anything about the Aimee situation, but we can still change the narrative. That means you have to be seen with someone—in public. A man, I'm assuming?"

"Okay. Yeah."

"Okay, that works. Let's see...I can have Santos give you a call sometime this week."

"Santos?"

"Yup, he's the most masuline it gets. You'll go to Lem's Diner together and be photographed at the entrance. For now—act like the article doesn't exist."

★⁺₊★ ☾ ★⁺₊

I do what Lucy has asked of me and get back
on-set with my head high. Days pass and there are no
calls from a man named Santos, no comments on the
article about Aimee. More photos are released and I
begin to cover myself with long coats and furs even
though Hollywood is not cold. For days I would go
mad over them, staring at my shape and being
sparked with displeasure until I realized I would be
more mad to dawn on something so silly and slight.

Delirah leaves a sheet on the desk, my name
scribbled at its heading. There are only three briskly
written lines. She moves on and speaks to the others. I
figure she has not read the article, or even heard of it.

I can imagine Marga in East Rey with the paper before her gaping mouth. Her eyes going wide, lips rising from their flatness.

The thought gives me relief. If the article is being read by the intrusive, those with blank eyes of greed and apathy, then it will not be read by somebody like Hal who has no time to spare for gossip or the pondering of a dull photo.

"I didn't know you liked *rockers*, Prisha Sule. Or women, for that matter."

Coffee dribbles down my chin, leaving me flushed, and I hastily wipe it away.

"I didn't know I did either?"

Opal Jones, the female lead of *Merrier Without Mistletoe*, blinks her doe eyes at me. "Sure you don't. I saw what *The Bubbly* has on you."

"All they have are misconstrued quotes."

"I don't know…I'd think it was a publicity stunt if it wasn't for that picture."

"Pictures are deceiving," I say last, and leave. Opal will understand once her time has come, this is her first movie, so she does not yet know the lengths people will go for a single click and read.

In an hour, three more articles are out. *Les-Be-Honest With Prisha Sule & Aimee Vare. Bombshell meets Punk. Rebel Barbie. A Witch and A Rocker.* My phone flashes in my lap. I leave it on a stool and go to my dressing room, wincing at the sight and breathing in the way of a gasp.

I think of those articles, on paper copies, digital copies, and audios, and imagine them burned. Eradicated. Demolished by flame. I imagine they will be forgotten, like my own name, and my breaths slow. My chest loosens.

I leave the room feeling lighter, as if the articles are gone already, discontinued hours ago. My lungs do not feel so short now and my skin is not so reddened.

As I'm walking back to speak with Delirah, I catch sight of a new plaque, on another door. It is just like mine, except the name on it is Hal's.

The male lead was supposed to be Rodrigo Feen, an actor from Brazil who is known to be picky with his roles and demand a cold brew with peppermint after each take. But the room is no longer Rodrigo's, it is Hal's.

At first I think it is reasonable, normal even, for this to happen. Hal has taken over because he is so famous right now and every director wants him in their movies, so much that they'd trade Rodrigo Feen, or maybe, maybe, it is because all I think about is goddamn Hal and I've drawn him here with my goddamn mind. Shooting has already begun. It would not make sense...but Hal might have had a sudden itch for Christmas movies and holiday comedies. A yearn that went without reason. It would not matter though, how it happened or why, because *Hal is my co-star.* We would act on the same set and have our names spoken in same sentences. We would be in a movie together.

"Prisha!" Delilah appears, eyebrows risen over the flush of already-pinkened skin.

"Where have you been? We need to shoot your scene with *Hal Moulin*. He's here. We've all been waiting for you on-set like frozen bags of—"

"Coming. Sorry. I'm coming."

We walk past the curtains where the room has gone hectic. There is movement as well as there are voices.

Hal stands in the middle of it all. His eyes are shut and he is perfectly still as a teenage boy applies blush onto his cheeks.

"I'm here," I say quietly. "Sorry."

Hal's eyes flash open. The boy steps away but does not move his sights from Hal's cheekbones.

"Oh, Sule. Hi."

"Hi."

"I didn't know you were playing Rhian."

"I'm not," I take my place beside him and face the crowd. I'm shaking, my fingers and the slightness of my legs, but I act with nonchalance as I stare at Delirah and smash my lips together so the lipstick will spread.

"I'm playing Tarah, the side piece."

"Oh," Hal grins, but he is tired, I can tell, and *not* trembling. "So we only have, like, one minute of screen time together. And we don't even really interact," He flits his hand. "Delirah was acting like—"

"Everybody! Places!"

"Hal, you're by the door. Prisha, you're following him out the door!"

"Okay, alright. Wait—Sule, I'm leaving right after this shot. Can you come over later?" He rubs his eyes, red blooming beside them. "At around 8?"

"Over?" I ask, and frown even though I do not mean to.

"Yeah."

"To your house?"

"Opal, come on this side, please. Near Prisha."

"Yeah. If you can, of course."

My head bobs. I catch my breath and say, "Alright."

He nods back, "Alright."

His eyes are on mine until Delirah comes between us, arms waving above her head.

By lunchtime our throats have gone dry and our shoulders fall forward in their tire. The break will only be twenty minutes long and the line for the craft service table has drifted off to the bathrooms. I am halfway to the tables when I see the darkened coffee and apple slices with peanut butter. That is all.

Hal walks past the line, a cup of coffee already in hand. He nods and says something to Christo DeCada before somebody comes and hands him another tall, steaming cup.

"For Vivian," They say.

"Ah, thank you so much, Konnie. She'll be pleased."

I turn my body, so much that I may not hear any more. But I do. I am looking at the pale apple slices, thinking that maybe I'll drench them in peanut butter. I inch forward, away from Hal and Konnie, but still hear when it is insinuated that Vivian is always on-set with Hal. That she is always in his room or trailer so they can spend breaks together.

I get out of line and read the script again. I am no longer hungry.

CHAPTER NINE

In all of the roles I have played, nerves are shown in the wringing of a wrist or the bite of a lip. There are loud breaths and hints of shyness within them, eyes lingering on dull spaces and fingers tapping—but I do none of this. It is worse—what I do is worse.

I sit still with my legs crossed and make a face that always makes my cheeks go numb. I think so many words and make sentences in my head, but I never say them aloud.

We were let out at 7pm, and by 8, Hal and I are in his living room.

He sits with his back to the wall, curls falling by the tilt of his neck. I talk, he nods, and we write. I keep the papers before my eyes, my fingers wrapped tightly around the pencil. He mentions the weather, the indecisive director, and the attention strays from him like children at the sight of costless candies—I lure it back. I would have jumped at this before—a chance at conversation, I did at first, but then there is an aching echo of a voice in my mind and I feel myself go somber. I remember the talk of coffees and blondes and breaks, and feel my body fall from its spirit.

"Maybe we should—maybe we should pick up tomorrow."

"Oh, okay."

"I'm not prepared."

"Ah, alright," He nods. "That's fine. We can meet tomorrow."

"I just need time. To read over my notes, and..."

"No, yeah, I understand—"

I rise from where I sat, quickly, and stumble beside the dining table.

"Sule," He says, as if his word is a steady hand.

"Yes?" I say, because it is.

"I understand if this is...hard. I have been told it is."

I nod. I am sure he means his mere presence, so I do not ask.

"I just want to learn from you. To improve myself. And we can do it any way you'd like, so long as you're comfortable. So if you need time, or, whatever it is you need, I can do that for you."

I nod. I do not say anything until I say, "Alright."

"I'm serious, whatever you need."

"Alright."

"I can—look, I can close my eyes when you speak, if you want me to." He shuts them tight so his entire face wrinkles. "Does that help?"

"No."

"Ah, really?"

"Yeah, really. Actually, it makes this much harder."

"How so?"

I shrug, acting blunt. "Just a bit awkward."

"I can—" He turns, moving so quickly that I am facing his head of hair now. "—turn around and listen to you speak. Or call you from the other room. On the phone. Or write my questions on a sheet of paper and toss—"

"Alright, that…I see. I get it."

He sways back around, smiling broadly. "Are you sure?"

"Very. You're willing to do anything."

"Pretty much."

"So I can stay."

"Pretty much."

"No, I mean, I can stay. I feel—I can stay now."

He does not speak, only nods and grins, bowing his head at the seat I had just lifted myself from.

We are on-set together the next day, too. I am working with Luisa Bunez for an hour before we are needed on-set. I place the scripts under my arm and pull pins from my hair. Hal comes rushing up beside me.

"Again?"

I do not ask what he means. I say, "Tonight?"

"If you can."

"At eight?"

"Eight works."

"Alright."

"Alright. See you then."

Luisa looks at me and squints but does not ask anything, and I am proud of my secrecy. I do not give myself away—except for the smiling. That cannot be prevented. Not when he is so much of himself.

By 8pm, we are in his living room again with the fire kindled, a mug of coffee in one hand and a pencil in the other. He keeps the tip of led pressed to the journal's pages but they remain empty.

By the third night of this, we have somehow forgotten to bring the pencils out and instead speak over each other, agreeing and nodding and I am trying—but failing, to hold back my smile.

On the fifth night, I tell him we are going to work on raising his vibration, and he sits up at that, as if the bend of his spine kept him from this.

"Ok. Did you ever read *The Alchemist*?"

"Yes. A long time ago but yeah, I've read it."

"Are you an alchemist, then?"

"I don't know."

"Because you speak like one."

"Oh, god," I say, but it is a whisper. "*Really*?"

"I meant for it to be a compliment."

I shake my head and he grins, but bygone myths and tales come to mind. Slow spoken elders and dull tones. "Are you sure about that?"

He smiles.

On the seventh night, I learn that Hal hasn't had dairy since he was ten and cannot drive. In turn, he learns I add cinnamon to everything and prefer to walk than drive. He tells me about Haleena, his late mother, while grabbing spices from his kitchen cabinet, and says that all of his dreams are of her as he hands me the cinnamon. I tell him about Benji while stirring my coffee.

"Is he close to your parents?"

"No. Not any more than I am. Which I'm not."

"Only to you, then? He's only close to you."

I nod, slowly, realizing this just now. "He has friends at school, I think, but yeah. He only really talks to me."

Hal grins, tersely, as if he should not have. "That must feel special then. Right?"

I smile and agree.

I bring up his fifth film, *Bold Boys*, and he says, "That wasn't a stunt double, that was me."

"No…It couldn't have been."

"It was, really, it was. I had to plummet into that wall headfirst—" He says, his face holding a passion. I shake my head. "Nothing was edited in that shot. Nothing. Except the lighting, of course."

"No—"

"It was." He laughs, eyes dashingly bright.

"No, I would've known. I would've."

"Well, he did look like me, so, you couldn't have known."

Now I am laughing along, and thinking, *I would have known, trust me.*

"I was kidding, you're right. It wasn't me who—"

"I know."

"—that was a stunt double."

"I knew that, Hal."

"I would've died running into that wall. I'm never sure how they do it."

"Me either."

He brings up The Met Gala, he has been to four already, and I say I have not gone. That I do not want to.

"I tried to skip out once—*tried*, and everybody acted as if I'd personally wronged them."

"Well, yeah, that's different. You have to go."

"And you don't?"

"No. Nobody cares."

He laughs again, and it is boyish. "Yes they do. Kaden was talking about you on his show last night."

"Right. I heard...did you? Did you hear what they said about me, I mean?"

"Yeah," His fingers tap the ground, making the sound of a pulse. "Yeah, I heard some of it but—they do that to everyone, it just means you're famous enough to be talked about."

"It isn't true, what they said."

"Which part?"

"All of it."

I felt that maybe I should let it go and act as if what Kaden said does not matter, but I would lose more sleep knowing he had heard the rumors and I had not corrected them.

"She'll be at The Met, you know," He says. "Just so you know."

He means they will put us together: Aimee and I. Pave ways for our walk and force words to our ungiving mouths. They will do what they can for a picture and a fruitful statement.

"I know. I still have to figure out what I'm going to do about that…"

I consider, for moments, bringing up the blonde. Asking about her. About them. About how long they have been together, how they have kept it from the public eye. How they are able to spend so much time together. But he moves on, and we start talking about the Met again. How we wouldn't even really be there—but hiding behind photographers and art pieces and hats.

"I'll join you. Right behind the sculpture beside it."

"Alright."

"Alright."

"Deal, I'll be the one in the hat."

"I'll be the one in the stripes."

"You know—I've been wondering about something."

I blink, "Yes?"

Hal taps a sheet of paper, gestures with an index finger. "Everything we've been doing, I believe it works—I know it does. But how?"

"Right. So, it all begins with our belief systems. What we believe will happen, *will* happen. Same with what we believe will never happen...those things will literally never happen."

"But what about the people that say 'I never thought this would happen', and it happens?"

"Their conscious selves thought that...but not their subconscious. A part of their minds thought it was a possibility, and so it was."

"But...how do those things actually happen? The possibilities. How do they actually manifest?"

"Because on some energetic level, they did happen."

He tilts his head, studying me. "What?"

"So, everything is made of energy, and everything also has a vibration and frequency. Everything. Like our thoughts and songs and foods. So, whatever vibrations we have—that we're sending out into the Universe, are the same vibrations that we're attracting back to us."

"...Example?"

"Yes, of course, so, say we're excited about a house we want to buy but we can't afford it. But we're not really paying attention to that because of how badly we want it. So instead we only think about how much we love the house, so much that it feels like it's already ours—and our brains—or subconscious minds, can't determine what is real or not, in terms of the things we imagine and the things that actually happen in our present reality—so somehow the house becomes ours despite the fact that we can't afford it. It's like…it's almost like the Universe rearranges itself according to the vibrations we put out."

"Now, in your case, we've been changing your thoughts and words so that your subconscious mind will change its beliefs as well…because your preconceived beliefs were limiting."

"Right."

"And now we're forming beliefs that will put you on the vibration of your desires by feeling those fervent emotions that match. It's like we're tricking your brain into believing that you have what you want—"

"Before I actually have it?"

"Yes! Yes."

"So…feel like you can afford the house and you'll have the house—even if you can't actually afford it?"

"Exactly, yes…we're just using our thoughts and words to manipulate our current realities into the reality we desire. By just feeling like it. By acting like it."

"Okay," Hal whispers. "Okay." He sets his mug down, careful not to spill it over the floors, and begins to write. Leaned over, with his curls falling over his forehead and his eyes narrowed for concentration, I am thinking that I will never want anything as much as I want Hal.

★⁺₊★ ☾ ★⁺₊★

For eight nights I am in Hal's home. On the ninth, I leave early to be in East Rey.

When I walk in Benji does not say anything. He stands and pats my head like a young child pets a dog.

"Benji," I say, my mouth pressed against the puffing shoulders of his jacket. "You're taller than me."

"I always have been."

"You were five inches shorter than me the last time I saw you."

He shrugs, and I know what he's done.

"Nice. Well, it worked."

I look around only to see that the house is untouched, the only decoration is a cantarito. Brown, plain and rubbed clean. I wonder if they will use it as a cup or vase; for flowers or for coffee.

"You've been gone a long time," He says this quickly, in a joking tone, but I can tell he means it. "How did you let it get so long?"

"I just got so busy—you know."

"I know."

"So is Papà here? And mom?"

"Working."

I leave the coat hanging on the stool, the fedora sitting above.

"Did you have school today? How was it?"

"Didn't go."

My chin juts out. "You *didn't* go?"

"I haven't."

"What do you mean—have not?"

"I haven't gone in weeks."

He moves past me, patting his pockets as if he is searching for something, but he is not. He has done this before, and I know it is just an act. A distraction.

"*Weeks*? What? Why?"

"It's not for me."

"School—school isn't *for you*?"

"Nope."

I shake my head, gaping and frowning at once. I want to say that school leads to success. Education leads to a secure future. It provides. It will pay in time. But that would be a lie.

I do not know what Benji's goals are. And I do not know that schooling is aligned with whatever path he thirsts to follow.

"Then what are you going to do?"

"Don't worry."

"I'm not worried," I say. "I'm *not*."

"Then why're you yelling?"

"I'm...not. I just—I want to know that you have a plan...You have a plan," I say, firmly, in the way of a demand. "Don't you?"

"Yes, Prisha," Benji stops to place a single cent on the wooden table. He pretends this is what he has searched for all this time. "I have a plan."

"Really?"

"*Yes.*"

I feel my shoulders fall from their tenseness, relief welling in my stomach.

"Good. Now I'm actually not worried. Just, please remember to picture your des—"

"Desired outcome, yes, I know. I know."

"I know, I'm just...reminding you."

"Can we talk about something else?"

"Fine. Actually—I almost forgot." I place the sketches on the table and face them his way. "Look at these."

His eyelids flit. "You drew that?"

"Of course not."

"It's you, though," He stands above them, eyes almost closed in their squint. "Right?"

"It is."

The sketch has been drawn by a weightless hand. The strokes of paint and pencil are feather-like, sauntering across the page and leisurely in their form.

The girl in the drawing is taller, a more slender version of me in varying tones of purple and limbering sleeves. The gown is lean but has the tension of a corset. It is cat-like, cunning and nimble, but made for me all the same.

"You're going to be…Cheshire cat…but, *you*."

I nod, grinning. That is when I knew Antoni chose right. The design is more me than Cheshire, but still a cryptic combination of us both.

"What's it for? Is it real? Are you gonna wear it?"

"Yup, to the Met."

"The *Met*?" He frowns, "What is that?"

"The Met Gala. A show…I need to approve the final design but I wanted to see what you thought first. Before I said yes."

Benji skims the tip of his finger across the lips of the drawing. He smudges the red across my pencil drawn face.

"It's made for you, obviously. My only thing is…you need to outline your lips. Like, draw a smile on. Joker style."

"I'll tell Antoni that. Thank you."

"So how long are you staying? Are you going to wait for Papà—" He asks this absently, knowing they will say maybe one word to me. "And mom?"

"No. I just wanted to leave some things here for them. And to come talk to you."

"To me," He blinks, pats his right pocket again. "About the design?"

"About next year. About the next few months."

"The next few months," He repeats slowly, the words distanced from one another. "You're still going to do it, then."

I nod. "Yes, I am. Will you?"

He nods back, again and again, then says, "I will."

CHAPTER TEN

The Met Gala is bright—that is the first thing I notice. The second is my body and the way it aches. My feet have swelled already and the skin of my back prickles beneath the straps of my dress. I am thinking that I was not prepared.

I did not know it would be like this.

Not a museum, but a zoo.

People are lined up from the left to the right, forming a path for the famed. They all wear black, eyes bright against the cloth of their scarves.

One by one we will trail up the steps and stand around smiling as if we are enjoying this. Maybe somebody is, but not here. I look around and see mostly that they wring their fingers and glance down at their toes and take deep breaths. A name is called. A person is led forward by another, and a flicker of dread crosses the next face.

I stretch my fingers over the fabric of my gown and squint at the mirror that hangs above. There is a line of them; they have given us a chance to rethink ourselves, and I am doing just that. I stare, blinking rapidly as if the sea-green of my eyes will go away, but I know the contacts will last for hours. My eyeliner is dark and bold and menacing. And when I smile, there is no doubt I am playing Cheshire tonight.

I move forward, nodding hello to whoever stands beside me. It is almost my turn, and then I will be inside and away from most cameras. Most.

"Oh! Almost us!" It is Malik who has spoken.

She stands to my left, dressed as the White Rabbit with hauntingly red eyes and sprayed white eyebrows. She waves her palm at every videographer that walks past but does not say anything. The encounter is awkward, but on tape it will appear winsome.

Marion Williams passes us by, and I feel myself slightly struck with awe. I have forgotten, it is not just actors and singers, but athletes and all sorts of entrepreneurs. Marion is gone by the time I have thought to introduce myself.

"Prisha, you're going to walk up right over there. You're following…" The woman brings a finger to her ear, there is a mic there. "Aimee Vare. Go ahead. It's your turn."

I ask, "Who?" just as the artifact beside me trembles.

A singer's voice has summoned the bass, zealous in its beats. I squint as if it will help me hear better. It doesn't.

"Aimee Vare, she's the only one on the carpet right now…Aimee…"

"I can't."

"Vare…"

"I can't—"

But of course, I have to. Malik is on the tips of her toes now, looking over my shoulders and out at the cleared pathway as if she is eager to parade the carpet and wave some more. This has all been laboriously orchestrated. I had been warned by Hal and Lucy both, and still I did not give it enough thought. Aimee Vare is set to walk right before me, and we will be photographed beside each other for every eye in America.

"The rumors aren't even true."

"What?"

"It's—" The photographers tilt their bodies forward, leaning aggressively against one another. I know it then, I know it without even having to turn. "They're making—"

"What's wrong?"

"Hal?"

"Can I steal her?" He asks, his hands far down the pockets of a burgundy cloak. "For a moment."

The woman nods, "Okay," she says, fast. His hat is tilted down so you can only make out the bump of his lips, but she must know who he is.

"That's fine...she's supposed to walk the carpet...now, but..."

"I think she'll do it later, thank you," My mouth hangs open, but it shuts the moment he turns to me. "Sule?"

I nod, "Yes."

"Let's go?"

"Hal, you just—"

"Where have you been?" He asks, and I know it is only for the woman's benefit. We turn, him leading the way. Malik hurries forward and I am forgotten.

"I was..."

"Here," He says, blinking against the light. "Just wait here for a few minutes."

"Okay," I say. "Hal," I say.

"Yes?"

We are close, maybe enough for our hands to accidentally touch. But I do not move or else the headlines would be bountiful.

"Hal."

"Hal—you need to get on the—"

"Hal, over here."

Hal nods, but I am not sure who he is replying to. "I have to go back, alright, but I'll—"

It is too loud now to hear the rest.

"Moulin, here. Walk here."

He is smiling, readily, when he lifts the hat. The chants have become pleas, and we know it is because they want more pictures. They always want more.

"Hal, here."

"Here, we'll hold your—"

The hat is taken from his careful hands so his eyes are without a shadow. Finally, he has given himself to the cameras. I tear my eyes from him in that instant, just as he is walking off, back to the carpet.

There are more cheers. More screaming.

When I turn back, there is only one star on the carpet: The Mad Hatter, and there is a longing in his face, but it is not for me.

"Prisha, you need to—"

"Forward—"

"Here. Right after Mal—"

I move forward and see that standing off to the side in the murk of photographers with her hands at her waist is Vivian Astora. She is dressed as Alice in a pastel milkmaid dress and doc martens. Her fingers fly up in a fleeting way, a gesture for Hal's understanding only. He does it back, making himself smile truly. There is an uproar at this.

"Prisha Sule? Prisha."

I watch them stare after one another, smiling and nodding.

It is a nasty, wretched thing to be jealous.

"Over here!"

"Prisha!"

I give in, dully, walking up the steps, rising until I am stopped hastily for questions.

"Prisha, how is it working with Hal Moulin on the set of *Merrier Without Mistletoe*?"

"Did you and Aimee plan your costumes together? Did you mean to match?"

"What?"

"You're both dressed as the most humorous characters in Wonderland. Was that intentional?"

"What is it like being friends with Hal Moulin?"

"Will you be going home with Aimee tonight?"

"Are you and Hal Moulin close friends now that you're co-stars?"

"Are things getting serious between you and Aimee?"

I do not speak even though it will look badly on my part, but I am too determined to remain private.

Aimee is close enough that I can see her smile broadly for the cameras in a red and white suit, lashes longer and darker than ever. We do not look at eachother, do not even acknowledge the other as the interviewers pry and shout like they are creatures living off of our scraps.

Hal is still being photographed, he will be for another hour, probably. I feel guilt as well as gratitude, but it is not enough for me to go back and be there with him. He has Vivian to lock eyes with, to mouth soundless sentences to.

There is an after party, but I don't go.

I take off my dress, leave the corset and tights on, and go to Bub's Diner. It is like most other restaurants in Hollywood, but families eat here more than celebrities do. Especially on the night of the Met. There are plastic trees beside jukeboxes, ornaments hanging at the wilted branch tips, and pink spots of paint on the checkered ground. It is a humble holiday adorned place where I will not be discovered.

"Hi there I'm May, I'll be your waitress tonight. Would you like to see our specials? Or do you already know what you want?"

"Uh—" I take a clip from my purse, it is bent and cruel to the scalp but it is all I have. I finish wrapping a scarf around my head even though I would be scorned for doing so.

"Just a coffee, please. Cream and no sugar—which substitutes do you have for dairy?"

I blink up at her, hoping a smile will make up for what she has seen me do. She is young, maybe fifteen, and wears a layered white scarf. Through it I can see the red of her hair. It is brighter than mine and carrot-like.

"We've got 'em all," The waitress taps the menu. "Almond milk. Soy. Vanilla oat. Regular oat. Coconut and rice milk…and then cashew, unsweetened. Which would you like?"

"Either oat is fine, thanks."

"Course. I'll be back in a minute."

I am still staring at her when a minute passes and she is back with the coffee. It steams, smelling earth-like and creamy.

"Thanks, I like your hair."

"Oh, thank you. I dyed it because—" She is still speaking when the front door opens, but the wind chimes have been provoked. A boy walks in, stout and red-faced by days beneath sweltering sun. I feel my head turn, curiously, as I see a haze of something slinking from May to the boy. From the boy to May.

"May? That was your name?"

"Yes!" She blinks, looking down at her name tag, as if she herself is not sure. "Yes?"

"I don't mean to pry…really, but, is that your boyfriend?"

May's face goes bright. She looks to the boy, then back to me. "No."

"Oh—then I'm—"

"But we go to school together. He comes here during my shifts for a slice of pie, sometimes."

"Only during your shift?"

"I think so," She smiles.

I notice that since looking at him, she cannot keep her eyes on me for long. She is half turned, shifting her body so she will catch sight of him while we speak.

"Call him over, would you?"

May blinks. "Nicolás?"

"Only if you feel comfortable with it."

"Sure, alright."

May turns, beckons the boy. Of course, he is already looking.

"Hi Nico," She says, even though he is still across the room. His walk is a waddle.

Nicolás smiles, his ample cheeks rising quickly. "Hi May."

"Hi."

"Hello," I say. "I'm Prisha."

Nicolás blinks at me. I think he might know who I am, but he does not yet say anything about it.

"Can you both sit for a minute, I know this is awfully random but I can see—"

"You're the witch," Nicolás says, then looks at May. "She's the Witch of Hollywood, Mayley."

She frowns, but there is a gentleness in her.

"Yeah, Nico. I know."

I hear myself speak. "You do?"

"Of course," May grins. "You're the reason my hair is red. Except…I thought your eyes were brown. They look…green."

I am sure I look a fool. My lips have parted in their shock. It is the first time that I am flattered by the attention fame has gotten me.

"Your hair is red? I've never seen your hair," Nicolás says to May, but it is quiet enough for the both of us to have missed it.

"Can I sit?"

May looks at me. "Can we?"

I gesture at the booth across and sip my coffee. "...Please, do."

May sits first. Nicolás second. They make the space between them clear; May does this intentionally, and Nicolás is blind to it.

"Are you really a witch?" He asks, and May frowns, but listens hopefully anyway.

"Sure I am. I think most people are."

"Like...me, too?" May asks, her hands clasping and unclasping.

"Yes. Definitely you."

"Is that what you were saying earlier? Is that what you were saying you could see?"

"Well, I was going to say that I think you are tied. You and Nicolás. By the soul," I drink again and my throat is soothed. My heartbeat has slowed. The Met feels like an eternity ago, as if I had watched it from afar. As if it did not even really happen.

"I told you, Mayley. I told you."

"Did you really?" I ask happily. "Did you already know that?"

May laughs a light and pleasant sound as Nicolás nods smugly.

"No, he didn't. Not really."

"Well, basically I did."

"You didn't."

"Well I meant it."

She turns to me, smiling still. "We first met in the courtyard at Big Bear. We were on a field trip, and Nico asked me if we'd met before."

"We hadn't."

"But it felt like we had."

"Amazing."

"Yeah…I didn't believe it—until it snowed. The day it snowed, remember, Nico?"

"Yup."

"The last day in Big Bear. He asked if I needed him to hold my gloves. I asked what for and he said, 'you like to catch the snow'. But he couldn't have known that. We'd never met. Not till then, at least. And he was right. I did love to catch snow."

"And Mayley, you knew my favorite pie was pumpkin pie."

"It was the only pie Bub's had at the time."

"But that was the first time you made pumpkin—you never had pumpkin pie here before. Only that day. And it was the first time I came."

Nicolás keeps his eyes wide, as if he would not dare waste these seconds. And May does the same.

They are wide-eyed and sweet, childish yet long-lived. Their energies have converged, spright and clouding their bodies, clear yet ardent.

They whisper and giggle, and I see how they were not drawn together by appearance solely. In liking each other, they have defied the ways of society, and I am in disbelief seeing this. I wonder, if maybe, it had always been this way; people everywhere loving the soul before the incarnate, and my whole life it was only I who had chosen to see beauty as an equal to goodness.

"So what did you think?"

I laugh, flicking my finger between them. "About you two?"

Nicolás bobs his head. "Yes. Are we kindred spirits? My mom told me about them."

"Kindred," May says to herself. "What's that mean?"

"Do you know what they are?"

"I do…but I'm not sure if you're kindred spirits. I think you're soulmates. Similar, but not the same, and it seems you have shared past lives."

"Past lives," They say, in awed unison.

For half an hour more, we speak of soul ties. Then May, ever so polite, asks Nicolás if he would take our picture. He says yes, of course, and I realized quickly that he would do anything she asked. My telephone rings, but I do not pick up, and am sent off with a slice of pumpkin pie. It is the only kind Bub's serves on Saturdays.

I left them with my blessings, and promised to return.

★⁺₊★ ☾ ★⁺₊★

The night is one of mirth. Hal in his costume, grinning because he cannot be seen well, and Vivian in hers, making circles in her blue cotton, prancing and flicking her wrists.

As they dance, Vivian is remembering the mesmerizing cat Hal had cut the line for. She is frowning and forgetting her steps.

She is thinking next that she should not ruin the night, it is so young and so lively, but then she decides that Hal is the one who ruined it first.

"Did you sleep with her?"

Hal blinks, "What?"

He knows who she is asking about without having to clarify, and that is enough for Vivian to know she is right.

"You did, right? Like you fucked all your other costars."

They are no longer dancing. They are frozen with a flatness in the eyes.

"No."

"Tell me the truth, Hal."

"I didn't have sex with her."

"I don't believe you. She's over the house all the fucking time and you don't like anyone around when she is."

"She asked that of me. It was her one condition."

"Of course it was."

"What is that supposed to mean?"

"That you're lying to me."

"We didn't, Viv."

"Then—"

"We didn't."

"Liar."

"If you asked, I would tell you. You asked me and now I'm telling you the truth."

They kiss, but it is not forgotten.

CHAPTER ELEVEN

Shooting for *Merrier Without Mistletoe* ended on a Tuesday, for good, and I spent my last minutes on-set talking to Luisa.

She gifts me a burgundy coat, its fur creamy and supple like a homemade foam. We talk about going for a drink sometime, and surprisingly, I am quick to accept.

Everybody is doing their rounds, bidding goodbyes and exchanging numbers.

"Just let me know the day."

"Of course, of course. Hopefully sometime this weekend?"

"This weekend works. Maybe Sunday?"

"Alright—Sunday it is."

"But before then—" Hal appears. He holds his hands at his chest in mock prayer. "Help me."

There is a short thud as he gets down on his knees and his head tilts back ever so slightly.

"What are you doing?" My eyes widen. "What are you *doing*?" I repeat, and try to look away. But I fail. I am trying to do too many things at once. To react to this, and to separate Hal from his beauty. To see him as he is, without such a face. May and Nicolás come to mind, the raw bareness between them, and I strive for it so deeply that I try to sound callous when I say again, "What are you doing, Hal?"

Luisa spreads her fingers across her chest. "What *are* you doing, Hal?"

He looks up only to wink at Luisa, and then says, "Help me," to me.

"You're being...odd," I mutter, and make a face as if I am repulsed. As if I could be.

"Please, Sule. Help me, please."

"Help you what? Up?"

I stick my hand out for him to take, and he does. He holds my palm for a second before placing it back down at my side.

My eyes widen again and I feel a shock at how warm I have become starting at the tips of my prickling fingers.

"No, I mean—I need you to get something for me."

"What are you—but why are you praying?"

"Because I already know what you're going to say."

"Then why ask?"

Beside me Luisa's face is wrinkled with laughter. She is looking from me to Hal. From Hal to me. I shake my head so she knows I am just as confused as she is.

"You can get up now."

"Hear me out first."

"I think I'll still be able to hear you if you stand."

"I'll see you Sunday, love," Luisa whispers.

"Thank you for my coat," I say back.

"Of course, darling. Hal—your pants are white. They'll be stained if you keep kneeling there on the floor like that."

She takes off just as Hal is winking again. Then he is back to begging. His hands fall to his side, mocking exhaustion now.

"I've been writing everyday. Acting and everything. I even meditated. For two minutes. Doing all that you said to do—"

"Can you stand up already?"

"—but I still haven't gotten this thing that I want—and I want it really badly—"

"Maybe too badly."

"What?"

I shrug and his eyebrows furrow.

"If you're yearning for something it's because you don't have it. What kind of vibration is that?"

"That…is a good point. But I can't not want it so badly so can you just get it for me?"

"If you stand up."

Hal covers his face for a second, his large hands hiding what must be a smile. "Okay," He whispers, "Fine."

"Thank you."

"Quent told me my *grand-mere* left a letter. For me."

"Your grandmother?"

"Yes. But she didn't tell Quent where she left it and my father wouldn't possibly know where it could be. And I need the letter. I need to have it, so can you please help me?"

A feeling like shame swells in the pit of my stomach and my hands fly up to cover it.

He is asking for a favor, for something that I cannot give…but I will try. I will try before anything else.

"You want me to help you find the letter?"

"Yes. Please, Sule. Please."

"And you had to get on your knees for that?"

"To be convincing, yes."

"You could have just asked me, without the whole…"

"I didn't have to get on my knees?"

"Of course not."

"It didn't help in the least? Are you su—?"

"I'm sure."

He grins, and as his lips spread, so do his eyes. The circles beneath them have gone darker in the past days.

Even now, tired and pleading, he is the most beautiful thing. And I am reminded of May and Nicolás. I am reminded that beautiful does not mean good, and then right after I am thinking that Hal is good even then, without his beauty, he is still goodness.

I shake my head, ridding the thoughts, and agree again that I will help.

Since we are no longer filming together, I do not see Hal the next day. Or the next. But on Friday the phone rings. I jump from where I am seated, the phone at my ear by the second ring.

"Hello?"

"Hi. Is this Prisha?"

"Yes, who's this?"

"This is Santos."

Santos has a voice like the sun, that is the first thing I notice.

He tells me, slowly, that Lucy has asked him for a favor.

"Right," I say. I thank him multiple times, then I say the favor is no longer needed.

He says, "Alright. But I wanna take you out on a date anyway. Not for the photographs—we can go someplace away from all that, if that's what you prefer." He says it as if I have already agreed, and I am taken aback by this.

"Are you an actor?" I ask.

"No."

He tells me—in the same tone of indifference—that he was born into nepotism. I do not say anything, and he begins to tell me that he's watched all my films, but they are never quite as satisfying to watch as my interviews.

"You're nothing like the characters you play, that's all."

"But you don't even know me."

"You can tell a lot about a person through interviews."

I wonder to myself if Hal would feel the way I do now, that you cannot know a person through interviews. I wonder if he would say I'd never really known him at all.

"So, what do you say?"

"I…there's someone else calling me right now. Can I call you back—or, I mean to say—thank you. For the offer. But I have to go."

"Sure," Santos laughs. The sound is calm and gruff, just like his voice. "You can call me back."

I hang up, because I do not know why I have promised him this, and the number calling is Hal's.

"Hello?"

"Hi."

"Hi."

"Are you—do you think you could come over today?"

I go. Of course, I go.

I am at his doorstep in an hour, giddy and sad all over again. The only sound coming from the house is music, muffled by walls and not voices because he has kept his word all this time. He is alone.

"Hey."

The door opens, and the music is louder now. Two voices mix and curse in a lustful way.

"Hey," I hand him the piece of pale blue silk I brought. "This will help you find the letter."

He stares down at the cloth, one cheek rising, one hand hesitating above as if he is afraid to touch it. "It will?"

"Yes. It will. Keep it in your pocket and you will find your letter."

"How? Did you, like, cast a spell or something?"

"Yes, I put a magical spell on it."

"Actually?"

"No. Just take it, and you'll find your letter."

"Okay," Hal takes the cloth, wraps it around his wrist and bends forward to kiss my cheek. "Thank you, Sule."

"Sure," I smile, it is wistful. But my cheek is aflame. I have been an actress long enough to feign apathy, but this I cannot hide.

I picture Vivian in the house somewhere, her T-shirt drifting off her shoulders, her smile never faltering. I imagine her seeing us and not caring because the gesture did not mean anything. That is why he'd done it.

"I can't stay," I say. "For long."

Vivian would not be fine with it, I am sure. Not when I feel this way for him. Not when I would do anything for him to have kissed me and meant romance.

"Oh," He shifts and his fingers curl beside his neck. "Okay. That's fine. Thank you…for the cloth."

I leave and my steps sound louder, my lungs lose their youth. I stop walking.

I will tell Hal how I feel. Now.

It is this, half-said truths and insanity, or relief. Relief, finally.

"Hal?"

I rush back to the house, my hands back at their sides. "Hal!" I will say it all, from beginning to end.

He is there still, at the door, a look of languor on his sculpted face. I am about to call him again when somebody else does. A woman.

She is brunette and tall and has to be a decade or two older. I do not move, afraid for a second that I would be interrupting if I did, but then I see how indifferent Hal is to her, and how they are meeting for one thing only.

Suddenly I *wish* Vivian were here. Vivian, with her startling figure and colorful eyes. Hal takes the woman's hand. The look on their faces makes my blood go still.

They do not kiss, but I am sure they will.

The door moves to close, but I am gone before it is clicked shut.

CHAPTER TWELVE

It is hot enough to be without a coat, and cold enough to bear the sun on my naked back. When I am on set, I am told to lather myself in lotions with spf and throw the scarves I wore as a child over my body to hide from the warmth that will darken my skin. I have been told many times to prevent this, to do what I could to be lighter skinned. I know there is a privilege in paleness, but I still find myself acting as if I have forgotten my creams or lost my thicker fabrics.

All morning, I have been sitting on the roof of my home, letting the sun overcome me, but I cannot shut my eyes. It is torturous to do so. I have not been able to rest, because all I see is Hal and the woman and their fingers intertwined. I see things in my mind, things that I did not even witness. I imagine them together, in his room, their lips speaking more than each other's names. I feel disgust and envy and confusion. Most of all, it is confusion.

Luisa calls at 2pm, it is an hour before we will meet for lunch. I almost tell her that I cannot anymore, but distraction is what I need.

"Prisha, love, my boyfriend really wants to come along today, so do you mind if we make it a double date?"

I sit up, "A double date?"

"Yeah, just bring your boy and I'll bring mine."

I am wondering what *boy* of mine she is referring to, but I do not say it.

"Does that work? At 3pm, right? In an hour?"

I agree, and then I call Santos.

By 2:30, I am walking to Cola Cafe wearing a bell-sleeved top and knee-high white boots. I hear my name called, it is a voice like summer. I turn and put a hand over my eyes. It has grown hotter by the hour. The sun will give burns on skin today.

"Prisha Sule."

It is Santos. He is not like his voice. Not simple nor tame.

He wears all black, and even though his hair is buzzed, I can see the pale brownness of it. He is grinning, the black of his eyes showing sprightly against the gloss of them. He is more night than day, more moon than sun.

"For you," He says, and steps away from the car, handing me the bouquet.

"Thanks," I say, and my voice comes out shyly; I have never been given flowers before. I am sure my mom has not either. "Thank you."

They are red, so dark they look as if they've been coated in paint.

"So," He says, and then smiles as if he has not said a thing at all.

"So if you're not an actor, what do you do?"

"I sell narcotics."

I nod as if this does not faze me, but I am sure my eyes have widened. "Oh. So do you do drugs, then?"

"Not today," He smiles. "But usually, yes. I do."

"*Prisha*!" There is a laugh right after, a familiar tune, with heels against concrete coming with it. "Prisha, hello love. This is Cole. Cole, you know Prisha."

There is more laughter and the chivalrous bob of heads. Santos introduces himself, but he is looking at me all the while. Luisa glances at me, blinking, and I realize she is confused.

"Santos is a friend. We met through my agent—Lucy Von Rage, actually."

"Oh!" Luisa says, but her face does not change.

Later, she will tell me that she had expected Hal, and I will hastily tell her about Vivian Astora and catch myself making a face, reminded of the woman again.

"Do you know what you're going to order?"

"A lentil bowl, I think."

Most of lunch, Santos does not speak. He nods and shrugs, but does not eat or say much.

When Luisa and Cole leave the table—to greet others—he asks me, "Are you all right?"

"Yes."

"I feel like you're not alright."

"I'm fine. Just tired. Why—are you alright?"

"Yup, all good."

This becomes a game: the questions. But only once Luisa and Cole have left the table for another drink or another greeting.

It's my turn.

"Are you shy, Santos?"

He nods, smiling, but it is almost sleazy. "Yes. Yes, I am."

"Huh. I did not expect you to be."

"Why is that?"

"Because you're very blunt on the phone."

"I'm blunt now, too."

"That's true."

"I'm quiet around most people, I guess. Not around you, or, I'm trying not to be, because I actually care about what you think."

He leans forward, making a thud against the wooden table. "Sorry—see, your friends have no interest in speaking to me, because I don't seem interesting. I don't mind that, but I would mind if you saw me that way, so I have to talk to you. I'm trying—I'm trying to seem interesting. You know what I mean?"

I laugh, "I already find you interesting."

He smiles, and becomes more sun than moon. He is his voice now.

"Can I ask another question?"

"Always."

"Why haven't you eaten?"

"I've had anorexia for like three years and it's only been a few months since I started going to therapy for recovery so it's kind of hard for me to finish a plate still—especially if it has meat on it. The, uh, the illness kinda fucked up my entire system. But I'm fine. I'll take it to go, if anything."

I ask a lot of questions after that.

I take Santos to Bub's.

"Hi, May!" I cannot help smiling, my hands are clasped and I am leaning across the table. She comes over, looking bashful and full of youth in her smile and layers of striped scarf. "How are you?"

"Good," Her cheeks go pink. I can tell she is pleased. "It's good to see you, Prisha. I'm good…Nico is coming later."

"Cool, perfect. This is Santos, by the way. Santos, May."

Santos nods at May, "Hey," Then turns to me, "How do you, uh, how do you know the waitress?"

"We met here."

"Oh, cool. You've taken somebody else here, before?" He looks back to May. "Must be good."

"No—I mean," May smiles. "She came here alone. It is good, though. We have pies and dairy-free shakes. Everything's vegan, but it's all American diner style food."

"Only if you want something," I say, my voice low. "No pressure, but I figured this was a better option. If you're hungry."

"Thank you," He says, and nods before turning to May. "Can I get one of your shakes then?"

"Sure," She takes out a notepad, her pencil with its tip already pressed against the paper. "What kind?"

"You got strawberry?"

"Yup. Anything else? Prisha?"

I order the same, and then we are left alone again.

"What about your free time?"

He winces, but still he is honest. "I…smoke. Weed. Nothing too bad. I do modeling sometimes. If I ever want the extra money."

"Really?"

"Are you surprised?"

I turn to look at him squarely. He is tall, enough for the runway, and he is the only boy I have ever known with a jawline more prominent than mine. "No. Not really."

"And you? What do you do in your free time? Have you always wanted to be an actress? Oh, shit, I almost forgot to tell you, I grew up in Rey, too."

"You did?"

"Yeah," He sets his elbows on the table, he is closer now. "But the Westside."

"I thought you were from Hollywood."

"I was in a foster home in Hollywood, then got adopted at fourteen and lived there ever since."

"Oh…what—what was that like?"

"I guess it was—wait, I didn't even let you answer any of your questions."

"What were they?"

"Free time. Hobbies? Siblings? Did you always want to be an actress?" He is nodding his head, thinking of more. There is a lucidity in the way he speaks, as well as a feebleness, but I am sure that is his natural way of being.

"I have a little brother named Benji. He's sixteen now. And no, I didn't always want to be an actress…it was just always in the back of my mind, though."

"Are you close? To Benji."

"Yes…he's my closest friend."

"Really?" His eyelids raise, feigning surprise in their flit. "Not Luisa?"

"Nope. She's just very affectionate. With everyone. Who's yours?"

"I guess Paige. He was my neighbor. In Rey. We still see each other—oh, the nails," His eyes fall to find my hands, and he blinks at them. I think he might hold them.

"Is there a meaning behind the nails?" He clasps his hands like a child who has been told to keep away from the sickly sweet candies. "They're always the same color. Same shape and length."

"No meaning," I say. "But it's a comfort now, to never have to pick another color and shape or anything."

"Yeah, it's your trademark, too, so."

I smile, "I guess so."

"Yup. Can I hold your hand?"

I smile again, nod, and his hand cups my own. I am guilty when my skin still does not flush, when my stomach does not go to flames. But if *Hal* were to...

"What makes you happiest?"

"Happiest?" He asks, like the word is new to him. "I don't know."

"Oh."

"I just…I don't think I'm ever *really* happy or *really* sad."

"Never? How?"

"I think if I was really happy, then that would make other things more sad. Like my lows…they would be really low…if I was happy. If I had happiness to compare it to. Does that make sense?"

I nod, "It makes sense. I get it. It's just…really cynical."

"Probably. It is."

"I bet it won't always feel that way."

He is still for a second, and then his eyes brighten, and it is hard to imagine that he is never *really* happy.

"Where did you learn all of the magical stuff? The divination? Sorry—what did you call it?"

"No, yeah, divination. Manifestation....you know, nobody's ever asked me so many questions. About myself."

He shrugs, as if it is nothing. But we have been together for hours now and he has not yawned and his eyes have not strayed. When I answer a question, he listens and thinks and is eager to ask another in his slow, careful tone.

"Do you only care to know me because I'm beautiful?"

"No…" He is quick. "No, I…the first time I ever heard you speak was on the radio…it was a recording for some event. And I liked the way you talk. I like what you have to say," He nods, making himself unembarrassed—for a second he had winced in his avow. "And then I looked you up and Lucy's a friend of my parents so I knew she was agenting you, so, you know. But, I mean, you are beautiful." His teeth come out for a smile. "Obviously."

CHAPTER THIRTEEN

Hal calls for the second time in five days when Benji gets into the car. I turn the phone down and smile at Benji. He does not return it.

"You know how many people have come up to me this week?"

"Where? At school?"

He nods. So he's in school again. I stare ahead at the car filled streets to hide my relief.

"They come up to you for what?"

"For what?" He fakes a grin; it is frightening for him to do so.

"God, Benji, don't make that face."

"To ask me if I'm *your guard.*"

"*What*?"

"Yeah, they're asking me if I know you, if I'm a paid *guard*. Said they saw me in a picture. I didn't even know people were taking pictures of you now. Some idiots. Do I *look* old to you? I'm not even seventeen yet."

I make a right while laughing and say, "You are tall, though."

"Tall—yeah, not old."

"What do you say when they ask you?"

"I say I'm a Sule, too. Are you gonna get that?"

"Get what?"

Benji goes silent and I hear the buzzing again. The phone has twisted around, glowing a bright blue.

"No. I'm not."

"Alright—" Benji shrugs, and then he is staring at me, his face hardened. "Wait. It's Hal."

"…I know."

"Prisha, what—? Hal Moulin—You waited, like, all your life for this."

I make another right. In ten minutes we will be in the hills, and this will be dropped. But not now. From the edges of my eyes, I see Benji's head go from one side to the other, his lips parted with words on the edge of his tongue that he is too startled to say aloud.

"But—Prisha, the phone. You spent all that time—all that time you spent talking about Hal Moulin and wishing all this shit now you're just blowing the guy off like some—"

"He's a womanizer," I say this calmly, but my voice trembles still. "That means—"

"I know what it means," Benji says, his voice as wry as my own. He moves, slipping into his seat so that his body is no longer turned to face mine.

We are silent, but when he speaks again, in minutes, it carries a calmness, but it does not lack fervor.

"Fuck him."

I blink, and suddenly I see Hal. "Would you say it to his face?" I feel a laugh rising, a panicked one. My teeth have come against each other, my cheeks flushing quickly.

It is a wonder that Benji does not see this—or Hal, even.

He lifts his shoulders, his face holding a flatness. "Right now, yeah. Probably."

"Well—perfect—I guess you can then."

We pull into the driveway and I hear Benji's gasp of breath. Hal moves aside. He keeps his hands over his head, blocking the sun from the brown of his blinking eyes.

"Is that *him*?"

I could say that I do not know, that I cannot tell here beneath the bright yellow of the sun, but even Benji knows that would be a lie. Hal will never be unknown by my eyes. Never forgotten by my forgetful mind or unforgiven by a tireless grudge.

"Yes. It's him."

"Did you invite him over?"

"Benji," We are parked, but I have not yet touched the door handle. "Why do you keep acting like I'm stupid?"

He nods, as if to say, *fair.* "Then what is he doing here?"

"I don't know."

Hal meets us beside the car.

"Hi, Hal." He is smiling. I remind myself to do the same.

"Hi."

"What are you doing here?"

"I called but you…Is this, uh," Hal nods at Benji, his eyes shifting from me to Benji and back. "Is this Benjamin?"

"Benji," Benji moves to stand beside me. "Who the fuck are you?"

I gasp, but it is soundless.

Hal coughs to cover the surprise that has flitted across his face—maybe because of Benji's language, or maybe because it is rare for somebody to not know him by first name and last.

"I'm a friend of Prisha. We work together," He looks at me, nodding. Benji says nothing. I keep myself from laughing—and scolding. "She's talked a lot about you."

"Right, yes, this is Benji," Despite everything, I wish I could have at least run a hand through the ringlets of my hair. "What, uh, what are you doing here?"

"Just…cold season and you weren't picking up so I thought maybe you were sick, that's why you weren't picking up. But no, you look perfect. In perfect condition. So, I guess—"

"You think I would have let you see me sick?"

"No, true. True. You're too altruistic to risk getting me sick."

I laugh, "I'm not, because that's not what I meant. But anyway, I'm not sick. Did you…" That is when I look down and see the book wrapped in bohemian cloths, and above it, a jar of thickened, bubbled honey. It will be sweet, I can tell, and made to soothe the throat.

"What's…all that?"

"I really did think you were sick," He shrugs and Benji sighs from beside me, loud and overlong. "Vivian's brother has a cold, so I just thought maybe you did too…Anyway, it's just a book and honey and some other things. My *Maman* used to make me eat honey when I had a sore throat but you can use it for anything. Anything that needs sweetener. I'm sorry I just showed up, I didn't expect—"

"You made me a care package?"

Hal holds his hands behind his back, hiding everything. "I also just wanted to thank you in some way. It's a small way, but I'm thankful you've helped me all this time and...yeah."

"Thank you, Hal."

His head shakes, Benji's along with it. I pull my fingers into my palms so that I don't rush up and hug him.

"Thank you. You didn't need to give me anything, really. What—what book is it?"

Hal's eyes flicker to Benji's as he leans over to place it in my arms. I take it, grinning.

I was wrong, what I said, about not being a fool. In these minutes, all is forgiven. Swiped from my mind by a skittish voice, taken so feasibly with a gift wrapped in vibrant fabrics. He does not even mean to be so kind, I know, but it slips out, his soul with it. The sing-song tone of his voice and quick-witted replies to questions. I realize it was not Hal's beauty that made him seem good to me. It was never just that—but I would have preferred it. I would have preferred him to be wretched and careless, rude and repugnant. For him to have only looked like an angel and not obtained the qualities of one. And if it were the opposite, if he were to be without vigorous beauty, I know I would still long for him. I would still want Hal.

"Do you do this for all of them?"

"Huh?" My head rises from its fall, as if a finger has tipped it upward.

Hal says, "Sorry?" But he is not looking at me.

"The women you sleep with—" Benji nods, slips a pair of keys into a pocket and steps away. "Do they all get a care package like my sister's?"

I turn to him in my shock, and see the child he once was. I am shocked—again, at the darkness of his eyes. The focus, the satisfaction, the whisper of a smile.

"Benji," I say. But he does not look at me.

I turn back to Hal. I picture the gold of his aura. The energy he does not only wear, but embodies. I imagine that it protects him, soothes him. Benji's eyes flicker to mine, stolen from their darkness.

"You look confused," He says, but not to me. "Prisha is too, she thought you had a girlfriend, but apparently that's plural now—"

"Benji."

"I'll be inside, Pris."

He takes long strides till he is at the door and does not turn back. I say nothing. My breath has come tight in my throat.

I remember the euphoric seconds before this. I remember feeling better. Feeling adoration, not humiliation, for the first time in days.

Hal stares after Benji, his face giving nothing away. I put my face to my shoulder, my eyes shutting, stowed away.

"So," He says, blinking at a spot of space beside me. "Will you come? Tomorrow? To work."

"To work…" I breathe in and feel another wave of weary. I clutch the book to my chest, feeling its smooth binds against the bones of my collar. "Sure. Alright."

"Alright, I'll see you then. Oh, and the book," He is walking backward now, slowly, and nods at my hands where the book lies, the honey sitting above. "It's *Symposium*."

"You're setting yourself up."

I am in the kitchen unraveling croissants from their wrapping, letting my eyes trail the rooms. I am more aware of the house now that Benji is here; the bareness of it. The brown walls and floors that wear no decoration.

"He's doing it on purpose. The gifts and everything. He knows how you feel about him."

"*Now* he does," I heighten the heat and the dough crumples beneath the fire, folding in on itself—we like our bread flaky. "I never told him how I felt."

Benji comes to the kitchen, arms across his chest. He is older now, taller even. I am thinking that I do not fear him, never will, but I am also thinking that everybody else should.

"You didn't have to. He knows, and you know."

"Of course I know. It is all I know."

I breathe in the scent of the powdered sugar. The bread melted above crackling butter.

"Prisha."

"Do you want chocolate on them, too?"

"Pris, look, I know you…like…like each other, or something," He brings his palms up and rests them there for a second, covering his face. His expression is one of repulsion. I smile, even now. "But he's not a commitment type of guy."

"He has a girlfriend."

"Exactly."

"You tried to hurt him," I say, quietly. "Didn't you?"

Benji makes no expression, but I see the way his head tilts, thinking of a response, wondering what I know. How I know.

"How did you do that?"

"Do what?"

"Protect him."

"I don't know…" I shake my head. "The same way you tried to hurt him, I think."

He nods, "Makes sense."

I am surprised when I do not scold him. Instead I turn and wrap my arms around his body, and suddenly he is a child again. Funny and youthful and my own.

"You can't hurt everyone who hurts me."

"I can, though."

"I'm being serious, Benji—" I moved away. "It's…I didn't teach you to harm others. And about Hal, don't worry about that. Worry about—you. I know you're still too young to date—but when you're older. *Way older*—love wholesomely—with all of you, and do not make them look like a fool."

"Of course, yeah, don't be a fool."

"No, I think you should be…foolish. Be carefree. I just mean you shouldn't make *them* look like a fool."

"All right, yeah, I'm sixteen by the way, but yeah. Got it."

"Exactly," My face goes flat. "A child."

"Almost adult."

"You're dating someone?" I ask, because he has reminded me of his age. I knew it then.

Benji only shrugs.

"*You are*? But you're a baby. Wha—does mom know?" He holds a croissant to his mouth, showing he will not reply. "Benji. Does she? I'll tell you who I'm dating if you tell me—"

"Prisha, really," He says this with a mouth of dough. "You're *dating someone*?"

I'm not, but I nod anyway and think of Santos. I wonder if he would have minded that. I am sure he wouldn't have.

CHAPTER FOURTEEN

"Sule, Sule, Sule."

I pretend to be distracted by the notebook. It is orange and plain like a marigold dried. All of its pages are empty and awaiting the press of a pen.

"Sule…"

Hal has said nothing about yesterday, and neither have I. It is more odd what he does.

"Your hair looks—" He taps his own hair, his gaze remains on my own. "Pretty. The way you've done it."

I feel that maybe he is mocking me, but his face stays waiting in its mid-smile.

I squint and say, "Thank you."

"Sure. So what are you going to teach me, today?"

He leans forward, one elbow on each knee.

I do not look up from the notebook. Instead, I take a pen and write the word *meticulous* at the top of the page.

"What're we talking about?"

"Today," I say. "We're talking about being meticulous."

"Meticulous," He starts. "I know you think so highly of me and all, but listen, I've no idea what that word means."

"Yes, that is a real shocker."

"Sule, are you being *sarcastic*?"

"Meticulous means to be detailed. Careful. Precise."

"Alright."

"Alright, so think of the Oscar, right now. Okay?"

"Okay," He nods like a child. He is giddy today, and I am confused by it.

"Now, do you want to win an Oscar in 50 years?"

"...No?"

"When do you want to win it, then?"

"I don't know. As soon as possible, I guess."

"It doesn't matter?"

His head tilts slightly as if he is trying to see whether I am tricking him. I am.

"It does matter to you. Doesn't it?"

"Yes. Right. It does. I was thinking that."

"You should be."

"I was…well, it crossed my mind. It did."

"Hal."

"Yes?"

"You should know what your goal is."

"I do."

"And be meticulous about it. You have to be sure about what you want. Be so detailed that it feels like it's already yours."

"Detailed? What do you mean by that, exactly?"

"Things like…like when do you want the Oscar? What day? Time? Age? Do you have an idea of that?"

His mouth tightens and his eyes roam in thought, "I do," He says. "I know."

"Good. You don't have to be obsessively sure about it or anything, you should just be focused on the possibility of what you want." I set the notebook before him. Hand him the pen, and pretend to ignore the slight graze of his fingers as he takes it from me. "Just think about what you *do* want. Always think about what you *do* want, not what you don't want."

He nods and nods. When his pen meets the paper, it is filled easily and faster than ever before. He writes about the Oscar and what that will mean for him within the industry.

He is meticulous and definite. If there is one thing Hal Moulin knows, it's how to improvise.

Dustin is silent, but moves her body this way and that. Crosses her legs, then uncrosses them. Rests them above the velveteen rug.

"Wait, Prisha."

Prisha blinks, pulled from her own trance. "Yes?"

"He didn't bring it up? He didn't say *anything* about it?"

"He acted as if it hadn't happened."

"But...he had to have heard what Benji said, right? He was standing right there, beside you both. Right?"

"Yes, he was...I was sure he heard, but then I couldn't understand why he would ignore it, and go on knowing that I liked him, I mean, I was jealous when I should not have been. I had no right to be. And just—it didn't make sense to me why he would still have me over but never instigate anything sexual like the way he did with many other people...Of course it could just be he wasn't attracted to me and wanted to be friends. Just friends, but I...I sound..."

Prisha stops herself and stares at the ground with a face of embarrassment. After all this time, she still does not understand why Hal acted that way.

"I sound crazy, I know, but he did not treat me the way you treat a friend you have no romantic feelings for. It didn't feel platonic…and I know it sounds hopeless, but I saw the way he treated his friends—our coworkers or his help, and he never acted so quiet and solely polite around me the way he did with them. And then when he asked me to move into his house? It just didn't make any sense. It never felt—"

"What?" Dustin blinks again, shocked. "He asked you to move into his house? When did he ask you to *move in*?"

She leans back with her shoulders pushing against the linen sofa and thinks of all the interviews she ever watched with Hal Moulin in them. The movies, the books, the tales and rumors. His sweet and composed words, and she realizes how even then, with all that content, you will never truly know a person through the media.

"Thank you for having me, Hal." I stand. It is how I end every session: with thanks. Hal shakes his head at me when I do so, as if there is nothing to thank.

"You're leaving already?"

"Yeah. Before it gets dark."

"You don't have to," He says, writing still. "If you don't want to."

I laugh, "Okay." But he shrugs, and I realize there had been no amusement in him as he said it. "What do you mean?"

"I mean you don't have to leave. You can stay."

I freeze, my hands caressing the papers, my feet flat in their placement.

"There's a room for you here."

"I know…you have lots of rooms."

"No, I mean, there is a room here made for you. Since I'm only available at night, usually, it would make sense for you to just stay sometimes," He stands and gathers the papers, holding them to his chest. "So you're free to stay anytime. Now, if you'd like. It's in the third hall, second door to the left." He pulls the door open, enough to slip out. "See—"

"Wait—" I shake my head and hold my palms out before me. "Wait, Hal—I can't just...I'm taking care of Benji right now and I don't think..."

"You don't have to," He says, his voice a whisper. "But just take a look, and if it suits you..."

He leaves, and for minutes, I stay.

I sit on the marble and do nothing.

I would not accept the offer, even if I really wanted to. I do want to. But I would not. So I rise and go to the front door, but then suddenly I am turning back around.

The walls of the corridor are bare, marble like the grounds and polished, too. It is silent, almost entirely, except for the muted hum of music close-by. It plays past the thin of the walls, making a croonful echo in the halls. A door opens, shuts, and I think maybe I'll run into Hal. I will tell him again that I cannot stay, and turn back around toward home.

But then Vivian Astora comes around the corner.

"Oh?" She says, thin boned and taller than I remember, wearing a white shirt and shorts that I will later realize are Hal's.

"Hi," I say.

"Hi," She stops walking for a second, stares at me blankly before saying, "Goodnight."

I bow my head shyly, and realize it is not nerves in me—but shame. "Goodnight."

I watch her leave, the small curve of her hips moving easily. I wonder if she knows about Hal being with other people. I see the woman again, in my mind, as if she is prowling the halls beside us. Her gaunt cheeks and peckish eyes low with age and a casualness because she knows the way to Hal's room with her eyes shut. Vivian's steps falter until she is no longer in the hall and I can hear the drifting of her humming without a care, and I am sure then that she does know.

We are both fools. We would prefer to have half of him than none.

It is only seconds later that I pass a room with a green door ajar. I see a whirl of smoke coming from it. A proud scent of dried herbs and cleanliness.

I go inside.

★⁺₊★ ☾ ★⁺₊★

In the morning, I am in the room again. I see its windows and silks and patterned pillows. There were other decorations too, ones made by a heedful hand and crafted by impassioned fingers. Small golden carved elephants and drools of beads, crystal balls with their sides rubbed till their shine shone through.

"Thank you, Hal, really." I say, my teeth showing brightly. I thanked him, again and again, but he would not hear it.

Hal, I've learned, does not take compliments or gratitude or flattery. He blinks rapidly and shakes his head. All denial, no acceptance.

"Most of the furniture in there is my favorite color, actually. The tapestries are all woven so prettily but I couldn't find a tag and I want to know where they're from. My father would like them, I think…And the lights, they're all yellow. I love yellow light, I'm not sure—"

"I know."

"—I ever told you that—and I thought the flowers were fake because they're just so perfectly cut and bloomed but then I smelled them and realized that they were real—"

"You shouldn't thank me."

"But you had somebody do it for me, right?"

"Yes, but I—"

"Then I do have to thank you."

"But—no, I didn't do anything, so—"

"Just accept it Hal. Thank you, thank you, *thank you, thank you, thank you, thank*—"

"Jesus," He puts his hands up in mock surrender. "Fine, fine, alright. You're welcome." He is smiling all the while.

"Good. Here," I put the letter on his knee and look away because I do not want to make a big deal of it. "Now, are you ready to manifest?"

"Yes, thank goodness. Anything but—"

"Being thanked?"

"Is that what that was? If so, yes, anything but…what's this?" He looks down and lifts the envelope from his suit. His eyes grow wide as he turns it over, the slenderness of his fingers flipping it like a feather.

"Read it later."

"What is it?"

"Later," I grin so wide my face feels faint, and when he smiles back the same way I tap the page swiftly. "Okay, so, anyway, now that you are very clear on what it is you want, you must carry yourself as if you already have it. This part will be *easy* for you."

He shakes his head to disagree but this is not a problem, because really, he knows it will be easy.

"Just act as if it is already your reality. You already won the Oscar. It's in your bedroom as we speak."

"But it's not."

"Well it won't be if you believe it won't be."

"You're saying that if I just believe something is real it will be real?"

"That's what I've *been* saying."

"True…it just…" He makes his neck long, curving his head like a bird's. "I'm still confused about the believing part. How it will change things."

"It'll only change things if you believe that your mind has the ability to change things."

"Isn't this just…wishful thinking?"

"It's more than that, but wishful believing, sure."

"I can't do this."

"You can. I did. I've been doing it forever." *It's what got me here.* "We can just try something else, first. Another method. We can continue scripting, we can use the placebo effect—ah, affirm. We can practice affirmations."

"Like chants?"

I smile. "No."

He opens his mouth wide, as if he is mimicking what it would be like to chant.

"No chanting. Unless…if you'd like—"

"I wouldn't like," He grins. "I wouldn't."

"Good. Me neither."

"Once, in *Thrash By Megan,* I had to chant the same words over and over and I lost my voice the first day and Dan didn't even get the shot he wanted so for five days after I was living off of chamomile and honey."

"Meggy?"

"*Yes*, Meggy. I refused to say that word for months after shooting. Hey, you watched that movie? *Thrash By Megan*?"

"Mmhm, it's one of my favorites."

"Really?"

"Yes. I watched it twice in theaters."

"You're serious?"

"'*Meggy, I like your attitude.*'"

"I liked that line, I just didn't like saying it."

"It's a funny line."

"That must have been expensive," He shrugs but shows his interest. "The theater, twice."

"Yeah, probably, and I would've paid whatever price to watch that movie, but actually, I got in free."

"How?"

I smile widely.

"Really?" He begins to smile back, all teeth shone. "Seriously?"

"Yes. I just expected that someone else would happen to pay for me, or somehow I'd get in free. I wasn't sure how yet, I just showed up the night it came out and a week later."

"What? You swear?"

"Yup. Both times were free."

"You're cool."

"Cool?"

He looks away but nods at me. "Yes."

"Thank you. That's the nicest thing anyone has ever said to me."

"What? No it isn't."

I nod, laughing. "You can't possibly know that."

"But it isn't. You've probably been complimented all your life."

"*That* is not true. And nobody's ever called me cool."

"But they've called you other things. More *creative* things."

"Hardly, but anyway, cool is my favorite."

"That's crazy. I'll be sure to call you cool more often, then."

"Cool."

"Cool."

"That reminds me—did you find your letter?"

Hal grins, "Why does being cool remind you of the letter?"

"Because it would be cool if you found it already."

"It would—it is. I did. Find the letter, I mean. I have it."

"From your grandmother, right?"

Hal looks down, as if our work is suddenly very intriguing. "Right." He squints, and I realize he does not want to talk about the letter.

"So, affirmations," I say, looking back down at our journals stacked messily with pages torn from their binds. "Let's see what you wrote down that you want. Then we'll just re-write those sentences into present tense statements. So, like, rather than saying 'I want' you will say 'I have' or 'I am'. Good?"

"Good."

"Then you'll say them aloud. Tomorrow."

"Alright—Sule?"

"Yes?"

"Do you want to see the letter?"

"Okay…" I nod. "I do, if you're comfortable with it."

He nods yes and pulls the letter from his pocket. It is already laminated. The first word I see is "*Mon*", then Hal. *Mon* Hal. My Hal. I look at him, but he is staring at the ground with his lips sealed a bright white. The rest of the letter is written in English.

Mon Hal,

When you read this I am in France, where I do not feel so insane. I know you understand this but I am regretful still. I do not want to die with regret. You are the only person who has ever made me proud. Keep making me proud.

- *Ta Grand-mere*

I look up again, and Hal is still looking at the same spot on the ground. I am not sure what to say, but what comes out is said firmly.

"I'm sure she is. Proud, I mean."

"I hope."

"Were you closer to her than your parents?"

"No...I don't think so," He smiles, shrugs. "But I liked her more."

CHAPTER FIFTEEN

The next day Hal smiles even more—he is happier. This is the reason why I do not understand how he is also more stubborn.

"I can't say it."

"But you can."

"I can't. It feels like I'm lying. Like I'm a fraud. I feel that often enough as it is."

"Then act."

"What?"

"Use your acting skills. Act as if you mean what you're about to say."

"But…"

"C'mon, Hal. Say it. You're an actor."

"God, no. I can't."

"Why? They're just affirmations—and the more you repeat them to yourself the more you'll really believe them."

"…No."

"Is this actually what you want, Hal? Is this what you *really* want?"

His face goes flat, the banter falling from its humor. "What do you mean?"

"Is this what you want most? Is this actually your goal? Is the Oscar really that important to you?"

"Yes," He is quick to say yes again. "It is," Then, "Why? What would be yours? What's yours?"

"Mine?"

"Yeah, your goal," He frowns to himself. He is so pretty when he frowns. "What is it that you want the most?"

I do not have to consider this. It is all I have ever thought of. All I have ever worked for.

"I don't know."

"Really?"

"…I guess I do. Maybe it would be to love someone," I try to sound indifferent; to sound as if it is only a simple, little craving. "And to be entirely loved back by them."

He bows his head, looks from my left eye to my right, then down and away.

"I think your goal is important," I say dumbly.

He winces, "In comparison, not really. It's something you can hold, physically. Not something you can feel. Not really."

"But they're equally important. Because it's important to you. And mine, to me. I only…" I breathe in, and then my words come rushed after that, in only one breath's length. "My parents never really talked to each other and it has almost always been that way, so I have always known what I do not want for myself. I don't want to live with someone and have kids with them and never talk to each other."

"But I didn't know what I *did* want, not then. And that's what matters, to know what you *do* want.

But then one summer, the drive-in—*Auraland*—they were playing a movie. I couldn't see over the fence. I could hear the movie, though, and I only heard like two lines. I don't even know what movie was playing, but from then on I knew what I wanted. Because of those lines."

I learned a lot by that fence. I spent hours with my back to it, pressing my ears to its cool metal. I was scolded often by the guards; I could not just sit on those private sidewalks, so I would walk past its gates and turn at the corners just to circle around and pass by all over again.

I would listen to the large crackling voices of actors and actresses speaking in the place of old philosophers and alchemists and leaders of renowned religions.

Through the bars the screens were a blur, but I almost preferred to watch that way. I liked to picture the films for myself. I imagined they all dressed the same, the men and the women and the others. I saw them in their long sleeved gowns, fabrics flush and fitting. One thing was said, and then another. All different words and ways of explanation, but in the end they all meant the same thing. All connected by a gist.

"What were the lines?"

I shrug and say, "I don't even remember," It is a lie, again. "But it was something about loving someone so much that you would reincarnate over and over again, only to find their soul again."

"But they would not look like themselves."

"Their shape or form would not matter."

"Even if they were an animal?"

I roll my eyes. "Even then."

"Really?" He leans away, as if he needs space to think further. "Interesting, then what would—"

"You're changing the subject."

"Wh—no. I just wanted to expand on the concept of loving someone without ca—"

"Do you want the Oscar or not, Hal? Do you want to be famous for your acting—your *talent*? Or do you just want to be a pretty face all your life?"

His eyebrows lift, his attention so easily swayed. "You think I have a pretty face."

I stare at him, my face a mask of awe. "Are you that dense?"

"Wh—how? *You* just called me pretty. I didn't say it—"

"I did, I know, and you're dense if you didn't already know it."

"Well, I knew it," He grins. "I just didn't know *you* thought—"

"You just won an Oscar, how do you feel?"

"I wouldn't know."

"Really? You're refusing to say it just because you feel like a liar?"

"If I say it, I *am* a liar."

"Fine, if you don't want to say it then there's no point in—"

"Alright, alright."

I fall silent.

"I'm *so* grateful for my Oscar."

"*Yes*. Yes, Hal."

"I'm—very grateful for my Oscar."

"You are."

"I am. And I am also—very, truly thankful for the letter. Your letter."

I breathe in, foolishly trying to mask my embarrassment with nonchalance. But he acts as if he does not notice and leans forward.

"It's funny, you and Chesca are the only people who have ever given me letters."

"And a million others."

"That's true, but yours…it made me feel…"

I look up again, my head hanging with a sudden impatience. *Made you feel what?* I think.

I ask it again in my mind, as if I could draw the words out from his closed mouth.

"Grateful," He finishes, but I do not think it is the word he planned to say. Or maybe I just wanted it to be something else.

"How did you know I want to move?"

"What?"

He taps his pocket, as if the letter is there now. I am thrilled that maybe it is.

"You mentioned that I should do whatever it is that will make me happiest...you mentioned France."

I nod.

"How did you know?"

I try not to smile, but I am glad I was right. France, where Hal would not be so restless. Where he would not have to hide so much.

"Your house. It's very French. You have their paintings and their architecture. I just assumed you'd want to live there. It seems like you do. And you were born there, right? In Paris."

His eyes wander from mine, taking in the house as if it is his first time seeing it. "Yeah, you're right. I would want to, but not for long. I couldn't."

"Why not?"

"Because…the people live differently there. They love films, but not ours. They don't care as much about the media and everything."

"That sounds nice. I'd like to live there, then. Somewhere like France, but with more nature. Something in the middle of that."

"You'd leave Hollywood?"

"Yes. For sure."

"But you'd be sacrificing your whole career."

"I would."

"Really?" He comes closer as if he will tell me a secret and the scent of cinnamon comes with him. "Would you sacrifice this for it?"

"No," I say, and my face goes hot. "Wait. What do you mean—by 'this'? My job? Here? Acting?"

He smiles. Nods.

"Yes, I would, then."

"Really?"

"Yes, I'm surprised you wouldn't...I can imagine you in Paris, you know."

"Really?" He asks again, but it is different this time.

"Yes. You would not be mistaken for an American, ever. You would fit right in. Perfectly."

He grins.

"You would go to a cafe in the mornings and have a coffee, but you'd stay there for six hours—working on something, and the waiters would let you. They'd never make you leave."

He nods, "True, they do not mind when people leer...Would you spend your mornings in the cafe, too?"

"No, probably not. I'd be at the park, painting or something."

"You don't think I'd be there, too?"

I shake my head quickly. And he agrees, grinning again. "Yeah. I would be too distracted, thinking about work."

"Right...so, when did you win your Oscar?"

He frowns and leans back into the cushions, the cotton of his shirt stretching across his chest. I lean back too, by reflex.

"March?"

"You don't know when you won your Oscar?"

"March 15th."

"Good."

"On a Wednesday. This year."

"Okay."

"I have to give a speech, I'm sure...for my gratitude."

"Right, of course. Do you usually write them out before or is it, like, spontaneous?"

"Spontaneous, mostly. But for this, I actually prepared a speech."

I feel my back rise from its slump and almost exclaim, "Really?"

"Yeah, it's not finished, but yes."

"That's perfect."

"It's really short though. Like, twenty seconds long."

"But that's good. If you read it now it would be good, too, for the purpose of manifesting the Oscar. If you were to act as if you already—"

"Read it, here? Now?"

I shrug, but I am hopeful.

"Okay."

"You don't have to."

"I will," He says, and I do not think he actually will, but he does. He recites the speech as if he has been practicing it all his life. This is how I knew he would win, without question. He would win.

"Okay…and mean it."

His fingers curl at his neck. They rest there. "Mean it?"

"Yeah, say it like you would at the show."

"Alright, so, then, first off, thanks to Quent for keeping me sane," Hal taps his head, as if he means this literally. "Thank you Hyatt Blues Studio and Agency. Thank you to all of America, my people. Thank you *Maman.* Thank you Viv, I love you. Thank you to Lucy Von Rage. Lucy, you are the reason I am here, and the reason I met *la seule personne pour qui je suis prêt à être faible.* Thank you *Grand-mere,* for everything—*tout.*"

For minutes, we are both silent.

Hal is smiling, but it does not reach his eyes. There is a sadness in them. I am sure it is because of his grandma, who he so obviously misses.

"No feedback?"

I gulp away the thickness of my throat and say, "You did perfectly. It sounded genuine. You should do it again, tonight. You don't have to act it out, if you don't want to, just visualize it."

"Okay. Thanks. Anything else?"

"Sure. You met the blonde through Lucy?"

Hal's forehead creases. He is confused. Silent.

I smile and say, "*Je parle français.*"

And then Hal laughs. It is real and sweet and child-like.

"*Really*? You speak french? *Really*?"

"Yes," I say, breathlessly, because he is laughing some more.

"Do you know what this means?"

"That I speak french?"

"No, no, it means you can come to France," He raises his hands swiftly, flung by his excitement. "You can come too."

"I wasn't allowed to go if I didn't speak french?"

There is a flash of pink as he runs his tongue over his lips and says, "Of course not. The Parisians wouldn't treat you well."

"Ha. Okay then, thank goodness I can go now that I know I would be accepted."

"Yes—I won't have to be ashamed that my friend only speaks English."

"I speak four languages, but *okay*."

"*Four*? Fluently?"

I nod.

"*Why*—Do you know what else this means?"

"No?'

"That you know."

"Know?"

"Ah," He laughs, lighter this time. "Maybe you aren't fluent. You did not understand."

"*Je fais.*"

"But *tu as mal compris*."

"Let's see. You thanked her, then you thanked Lucy for introducing you to her." Even now, after a year of knowing Vivian, I still will not speak her name. It is a shame that after all this acting I still cannot hide my jealousy.

"I didn't meet Vivian through Lucy. She's not even an actress."

"Oh."

"Yeah, I wasn't talking about Vivian."

"Okay."

"Don't you want to know who I was talking about, then?"

"No. Not really."

He flinches, if only for a second. "You don't?"

I do not reply. I am a fool all over again.

"Don't you want to know who I was talking about?"

"No. I don't."

"Why?"

My bag, across from me, begins to hum as if it has a heart of its own. The phone is ringing.

"I just don't."

I lean forward and click the phone off. But then I look down, and I see who has called. Hal glances down too, by instinct, and looks embarrassed at having done so.

"But why?" Hal asks, and he is different now. He has never acted this way before and my skin is flushed by it—so I put the phone to my ear.

Santos speaks first. "Hi. It's been a while."

"It has…How are you?"

"I went back to Bub's. I saw your friend and everything."

"Really? Did she…did she remember…you?" I ask, and look at Hal. He is frowning again, but away, not at me.

"She did, she asked about you—are you busy? You sound busy."

"I'm sorry. Sort of—"

"Sort of busy or sort of sorry?"

"Busy. I can call you back."

I can almost see Santos in my mind, nodding after I say this.

"Could I?"

Hal turns to me and he is different *again.* His doe eyes blink and blink, as if he is lost. The pink of his lips has paled, as if bitten.

"Do you really not want to know?" He asks, even though I still have the phone pressed hard to my ear.

"Of course."

"Okay. I'll call you back later."

"No problem. Call me later."

"I will."

I click, and then stare at Hal again. "I said no. I don't want to know."

He nods, leans forward, and sets a palm on the right side of my face. His fingers trail to the ends of my eyes, as if he would catch a tear there.

"Are you sure?"

"Hal—" I flinch and touch my face where his hand was. "You can't—" It is still hot, still burning. "You can't touch me like that. Or talk to me like that. I'm not one of those women—I won't be. You can't treat me like you—"

He returns to himself, startled and fraught, "You're not. How do you know—what women?"

"You know what women, and I'm not one of them."

"I wouldn't—I would not have you just to—"

"Then you can't act that way. You're seeing—you're with *Vivian.* And you know…how I feel, I can tell that you do, and yet you're touching me—it's like you're leading me on. You can't lead me on."

I gather my things, shoving them into the pockets of my bag and crumpling papers to fretful pieces.

"I want to explain," He says.

"Then explain."

"If I could speak."

I do not have to reply, my face is enough of disbelief for his understanding.

"I know I can, I, that's not what I mean…" He turns, so I can only see half of him. A jaw and a narrowed eye.

"There are things that I would say to you if I could speak."

"You are speaking."

"If I could speak to you." He trails off, unmoving now in position and word.

"What are you talking about?"

To this, he says nothing. So I leave.

CHAPTER SIXTEEN

It is the first time Hal has not kept his word. Today they will not work alone.

The room is full.

There are workers wiping already-clean desks and shifting chairs, making noise with a senseless purpose.

They have been asked to do this, to end and start again.

One of them whispers to the other, "Why is Hal writing things down instead of just...talking?"

"Why doesn't he just *tell her*?" Another says, "She's standing right there."

They act annoyed, and spiteful, but really they are feverish with gossip. They are excited to see the Witch in the flesh, and to know what the papers do not.

Hal hands a slip of paper to Quent. Quent makes his way across the room and places the paper before Prisha. For minutes, Prisha is scribbling down affirmations. She sighs, writes more, and her hands throb in their hurry.

"I wonder why they're not talking."

"It's so quiet when they're not."

"…yeah, can you imagine her right now?"

"Who? Vivian?"

"Yup. She's probably *very* pleased right now."

Prisha finishes, hands the paper to Quent just so that Quent could give the paper to Hal—who is standing a foot away now.

"Definitely."

"She's thanking God right now," Staci says. Staci has met Vivian only in passing, but she has worked at the Moulin home for years.

When Vivian walks into the room everybody straightens, keeping a watchful eye and ear. She looks from Hal to Prisha, from Prisha to Hal. They're standing on opposite sides of the room, and neither of them have noticed her entrance.

Vivian makes a decision at that moment.

Staci smiles without any real mirth, "She probably prayed for it."

Before nightfall, Prisha is gone.

When I get up, it is only for water.

The swallow and taste startles me, wakes me from the dullness I have been living in.

I hear voices, wisps of conversation. My name, and another's.

I remember where I am and who speaks so closely.

I remember that I could not bear to be alone, so I left Hal's for good.

But I had forgotten what it was like to be home—not in my Hollywood house, but home. I had forgotten what it was like to cry so often and love so much and feel guilt without reason. It is almost enough to make me pack all over again and bang on Hal's door.

Papà does not speak to me, barely even looks at me, but when the sun sets I can smell halloumi grilled. Papà is the only one who ever uses the stove.

Mom acts differently. She is not like Papà. She welcomes me but frowns as she speaks. And then she says I do not look like myself. Says I have become too entitled. Too white-washed. I wince and run my fingers through my hair, trying to make it less flat. I tell her that I changed myself only for acting roles and know that it is not true.

"Prisha," Benji says.

"Benji. I missed you. Your hair is longer now."

"You're back."

"Too soon?"

It has been a month since Benji stayed with me, but he has changed so quickly that I might have missed it if I came any later.

"What's going on? Anything…new?"

"Just working."

"Me too."

"I'm tired of it, though."

"Me too. Are you going to quit, then?"

"I don't know," My voice is lower now. "I think so. I think I'm going to leave."

"I know," He says this beneath his breath, with his eyes lowered so our parents would not pay us any attention. "I want to leave, too."

On my fifth night here I am too cold to sleep. Benji is beside me like a lamb, curled up and humming with the wind.

I do not know how much longer I will stay. Not just in this house, but this city. In Hollywood. It is no longer sheer glee and adoration to be beside Hal. It had once felt that way. To just stand beside him was excitement—gratitude and giddiness. But now, it does not feel that way. Even if he is in the same room, with his teeth flashing for a smile. He talks to the others, glancing at me every now and then as I do the same. But I feel myself fading now, in sadness, I realize.

For days I have felt this way. I notice the fall of my face, the constant thickness of my throat. Hal's presence no longer brings what it once did. *Change your thoughts*, I hear the voices of those actors portraying every soul of sapience. I hear them say *your life will change once your thoughts do.* I remind myself this; of their words. But only for a few seconds does the sadness fade. And then it is back again, and I am reminding myself—pleading with myself—to be happy. To move on.

There is an event, and I go, because Lucy tells me I have to. She is getting tired of my shuffling acts. I do not go out like I am supposed to, I do not feed into my witch-like persona. I have stopped painting the sides of my eyes with slim lines of white ink and dressing in long sleeved tops with a V shape at its neck. I do not smile in the way of a clever chartreux for the cameras or do tarot card readings on set.

Hal is always at these events. It is what he wants, afterall, the eyes and mouths that wait on him with bated breath. The words of approval and the brush of new lips on the high bones of his cheeks.

I enter the rooms of these gatherings and become surprised all over again by how numbed I have become. Warmth does not grow in my cheeks and I feel no need to gasp for air—until I see him. And then I look away quickly so the rush of my pulse will leave quickly, too. I would prefer the emptiness. I would prefer it now to everything.

When he sees I am there he saunters across the room, almost by my side. He might speak to the actress beside me or the bartender who has just handed me a short glass of wine.

It feels like a tease, a cruel game where he does not need to speak to show me he is not nervous that I am here or sad when I am not.

He talks to most everybody. He makes his rounds leaving stains on cheeks and giving advice when it is asked of him. One night he tries to make conversation with me. He smiles at me.

I cower away. I feel that I should leave. I should go someplace else, somewhere that I don't feel like I'm going mad wondering what is wrong. Hal does not love me. Is that all? I left because I could no longer bear wanting the one thing I could not have. But hadn't I said I would do anything to be with him—to just be near him? Wasn't that enough?

I used to think so. I used to believe I would do anything for that, for his mere company and nothing more. Even if I was a secret, something to be shamed upon. Hal would be the exception. For everything. To endure anything. But I was wrong.

★⁺⋆ ☾ ★⁺⋆

On March 15th, there are only two things on everybody's mind: Hal Moulin, and his Oscar.

When his name is called, the roaring begins, and it does not end for days. The light sprouts at his first step and follows him from seat to podium, the white of his suit becomes suddenly dull beside the brightness of his skin.

"First off—" He says, and the room begins to fall from its screams. Instead, there are clasped hands and flushed cheeks, whispers and giggles of adoration. Some streaks and some tears. They wait, but he only repeats himself.

"First off…"

He looks around, meets the eyes of Quent and Viv and Tie and Lucy. He realizes she is not in the crowd. Prisha is not there.

"First…"

Somewhere indoors, a young boy yells his congratulations—and Hal is snapped from his stupor.

"Ah, thank you—first off, to all of America, my people. Thank you."

The roaring begins again.

★⁺₊★ ☾ ★⁺₊★

"I want Hal."

This is decided by most everyone tonight.

"Hal Moulin," Diana says, as if his last name is needed. It is not.

"Doesn't everybody?"

"I'm serious, Rudy," She bares her teeth in a mocking way. "I want to be with Hal Moulin—"

"Don't you think you're aiming a bit too high?"

"But I'm gorgeous."

"You are hun, but look."

"At what?"

They watch him, together.

They watch as the sylphlike boy runs a hand through his dusk curls and saunters a few steps over until he is standing just beside Prisha Sule.

"At that."

"At *what*?"

"Can't you tell something is going on between him and that red-headed doll?"

Diana gasps. "The witch? She's a seven, at most." She looks around, her small mouth agape as if she cannot believe what she's hearing. "Or a five."

"…I'd give her a nine."

"No you wouldn't. She's too young. She dresses like it's Halloween everyday. And look, Rudy, her hair's not even past her waist. Hal wouldn't marry a girl like that. She was raised in East Rey, too, by the way."

"You think she's too young?"

"She's in her twenties."

"But that just means they're the exact same age."

"But Hal goes for older women."

"Forget what he goes for, they're connected."

"Hal and the red-head?"

"Yes," Rudy's face becomes excited. "*Connected, connected.*" He knows Diana will listen to this.

"Do you know Yalerah Eye?"

"The witch from Torraine? Of course."

"The psychic. She says they are connected by—"

"Connected? Like—"

"Twin souls. Twin flames."

"What?"

"Not just connected by the soul, but *sharing* one. A half and another half. That is what she called them."

Diana blanches, all mocking swept away in a breath. At first she will deny this, but it only takes seconds for her to recollect and realize.

"Of course," Her voice is barely a whisper. Rudy leans forward, his lips the shape of a small, perfect circle.

"You can see it, now?"

"*Yes*...I don't know how I missed it before...I can...*I can see it.*"

Rudy blinks, staring after Hal and Prisha. They are never more than a foot apart, their bodies always somehow angled to face the other. But they do not speak, not tonight. They haven't for three weeks.

"There's a...there's this light connecting them. Like a string," Diana says. "Even without lineage to witch blood I can see it."

"Where?"

"There, right there, you see?"

"Where?"

"Right there. You see it?"

"Oh, my god."

★⁺₊★ ☾ ★⁺₊★

CHAPTER SEVENTEEN

My Hollywood home is on the market by Monday morning. The people have spread word that the house was once mine, and it now carries the name "Covenstead".

It will be sold by evening time. I am making phone calls to different companies, agents, and coworkers. And then I call Santos.

"How are you?"

"I'm fine…I'm psychologically well," He says. "But you never called me back."

I nod even though he cannot see me, and even though we have known each other for so little time, I think I will miss him.

"I know, sorry. I've been busy. That's why I called, actually. To tell you that I'm leaving."

"Leaving?"

"Yeah. Hollywood."

"Entirely?"

"Yes. I'm moving away."

"…That could make me psychologically *un*well…"

"Sorry," I say. I can think of nothing else.

"Moving where?"

"Solana."

"What's in Solana—or…who?" He says. "Who. Right?"

"No…no, who. It's a few hours out of here, just an area I've always wanted to live. I'm taking Benji. I called to—I just wanted to say goodbye. I know it's not in person, but—"

"But it could be?"

I feel a sort of relief. Maybe I wanted this. Or maybe it is just a consolation that somebody does care. That somebody does want me.

"Yeah, it could be."

"Or I could visit you in Solana."

"You could, if you wanted."

"Really? You'd let me?"

"Of course. Yes."

"Alright, so then this isn't goodbye."

"It doesn't have to be."

"'Kay then. I'll see you soon, Pris." He hangs up, and leaves me again to wonder why he cares so much.

There are many moments after that, throughout the years, when Santos proves this to me. And again and again, I will ask why.

Why should he do so much for somebody who does so little in return?

And every time, he will tell me that I have given him a healthier addiction, that is why.

I call Benji next. He has rid most of what he owned, which was not much at all, and the only thing he waits on is me. He does not speak of Mom and Papà, so I am guessing they do not know of our plans.

Years ago this might have given me a thrill. That we are escaping, finally, but instead I now feel a pain so dark that I yearn to hold them once more to say goodbye.

Before we leave, as I'm helping Benji put his things into the trunk, I go inside and hug them, and I never once regretted that.

An hour later I hear about Hal. I hear about his Oscar, and know it is time that I go. But I will hear his voice once more.

"May I speak with Hal?" Is the first thing I say.

"It's me," He says. His voice over the phone is something I never got used to.

Raspier. Brighter.

"What happened?" He asks.

But I am quiet, shutting my eyes and committing the sound to memory.

"Is something wrong? Are you alright?"

"Of course."

"Oh—okay. Alright, it's just that you don't call much. Ever."

"I know."

"Prisha," He says. "Why aren't you talking to me?"

"We aren't talking to each other."

"I tried though. To talk to you."

"Once, and you acted like everything was fine. Like nothing happened."

"I know…but I don't know what to say. Am I supposed to—" His voice grows low, and I am reminded of how unfair this is. "Am I supposed to tell you I'm sorry when I'm not?"

"Why are you whispering?"

"I'm not."

"Because you don't want her to hear, right?"

"I know why you haven't talked to me."

"Do you? Because I don't even know."

"It's because you're scared. Right? Because you know I want to know you—more of you, and you don't think it's genuine? Right? I can tell because you won't tell me anything. You only show me what you want me to see—but I'm not just another person, Sule. You can treat me like a normal human being, you know."

"I talked to you more than I talk to anyone."

"Then why did you stop?"

"Because I wasn't the only one."

"You were."

"You've been with Vivian for years, probably, and you were spending time with me only because you needed help. You were using me to get *somewhere else.*"

"But I was always with you."

"For a few hours, and then you were back with her. And when you weren't with her or working with me you were doing god-knows-what with other people."

"But even then I was with you."

"That makes no sense."

"I was always thinking about you."

"Then why didn't you tell me?"

"Tell you what?"

"Everything you're saying right now."

"What?"

"Why didn't you ever *say* that you were thinking of me? It's too late now. You're telling me too late. And you're only saying it because I've practically left you with no choice."

"Because you wouldn't have felt the same before."

"I have always felt this way."

"But you would've stopped."

"Stopped? How?"

I almost told him that I'd wished to. That I'd begged myself time and time again to stop.

"You wouldn't have wanted to be around me anymore. People want what they can't have, and if I told you from the moment I met you that I wanted to be with you always, you wouldn't have felt anything for me anymore. People like the chase. They don't stay after that, they never stay for—"

"You don't understand then," I cut in.

"You don't. I'm telling you exactly what's happening: you left. You stopped talking to me."

"That's because I couldn't stay anymore."

"Because the chase is over? Because I touched you and you knew you had me, then?"

"Because I hate Hollywood."

He goes silent, but I imagine that he is somehow smiling at this. It is the first time I've said it aloud.

"I was only here for you and since I've accepted it's not going to happen, I'm leaving. I hate living here and I hate working here. I fucken hate it. Unless it's with you. And I called to just—only to tell you that I'm leaving Hollywood completely—I'm leaving the city. So I can't see you anymore, anyways, but you should know you never needed my help. You know your power, all you ever needed was to—"

"Sule," He is quiet, but I hear it. "Sule. Stop."

I stop. Because it's Hal.

"Could you come?"

"Where?"

"Here. Can you come here? To my house. Could you come over?"

"For what?"

"Just come to the main room. Please—Quent? Please. The door will be open."

The line cuts off.

When Prisha arrives, Quent is already at the door. His hands are clasped, held back along with his thoughts. He has wished, secretly, for her to come around again.

"Ah, Miss Sule. It's so nice to see you." There is relief there, in his voice. She can hear it.

"Oh, thank you, Quent," Prisha smiles gleefully. "It's so lovely to see you too. How are you?"

They linger by the doors for a few seconds. He bobs his head, tells her Hal has been waiting for her, and she says that there was traffic, like any other day in sunny Hollywood. Then they begin to walk, slowly, so that they may talk some more. Quent talks about the new piano in the foyer and the small trinkets that have been left in her room, but they both know she will never go back there, ever. Not once.

When they reach the main room, they enter together, but Prisha and Hal still do not speak.

He is leaned over the table, palms rooted against the marble. His lips move but he does not say anything aloud.

I made 2.5 million dollars on my newest film, The Passageway Plaza. I made 2.5 million dollars on my newest film, The Passageway Plaza. I made 2.5 million dollars on my newest film, The Passageway Plaza. Hal reads this, over and over.

Quent taps his foot. He's thinking, *get on with it, Hal.* Prisha grips the table till the tips of her fingers pale. She is thinking the same.

"You asked me to come here just so that I can watch you read?"

He doesn't reply, he just keeps reading. Reading, reading, reading. But not actually reading, because for a moment, his eyes widen and he thinks, *she's talking to me.*

"It's been like ten minutes. And I have to go."

I made 2.5 mill—

"I'm going to leave. Thank you, Quent." She turns. Hal does the same.

"I got the check this morning."

The room is silent, but Quent is smiling now. He is eager, waiting for more, like a child greeted with arms that bear candies. He watches them, eyes trodding back and forth.

"I got the check. This morning. Delivered right at my doorstep, like we said it would. Two point five million—"

"*Hal,*" She says. It is a warning. "Shut up, Hal."

"I'm being serious," He smiles at Prisha, he has waited all day to tell her this. "I have the check in my—"

"Hal," She says, her fists locking. "Stop, Hal. Are you lying to me?"

"Nope. No. I got *exactly* two point five million fucking dollars—"

"No way."

"Yes way. It arrived at 8 in the morning. On the dot, just like we said it would."

They are staring across the room, grinning, grinning, grinning, until Prisha cannot stay put. She rushes to hug him, and as soon as she pulls away, she has his face cupped in her hands. He leans into her and sighs the words, "We did it." Just as she is saying, "You did it, Hal!"

We do not speak of the past weeks. We don't talk about the future either. Not about leaving Hollywood or the amount of money in that check. We are sitting on his living room floor, leaning over two mugs of cinnamon sprinkled coffee between us.

They act as a barrier. They keep us from touching.

"No, I'm agreeing, records *are* cooler than CDs. The sound just isn't as good."

"What? No, you don't get it. It's better."

"*It's grainy*. And slow."

"But that's what makes it good. The fact that it's grainy."

"I won't agree with that. Oh—I had dairy today."

"*You did?*"

"Yup. I was on Sunset and a friend gave me chocolate," He says, and I know he means a fan. "She begged me to eat it and I said I would even though I wasn't going to but then she said she wanted to see my reaction…so I ate it."

"It was that easy?"

"I couldn't say no."

"Well? Was it worth it?"

"It was good."

"Understatement."

"Very true. Did you hear that rumor, by the way? About me. And you."

"Which one?"

"It was in a few articles. I think it came from a psychic in another city. She reads souls. Does readings, I think."

"No, I didn't hear it…what did she say?"

He shrugs, grins as if it a stupid rumor. Something impossible and foolish.

"What was it?"

"She called us twin souls or something. Twin flames. I don't know. It's supposed to be something like soulmates, except—"

"It's different," I say. "Much different."

"Ah, I thought you'd know. Which is why I was surprised you haven't read it."

"I haven't read much at all lately."

His face goes flat, lips sinking unknowingly over his chin, but I am thinking too much of what the psychic has called us to ask what is wrong. It makes sense to think of us this way, as mirrored souls that are said to never last.

"That's nice though. Not everybody has a twin flame."

"You don't think so?"

"No."

He shrugs at me and says so randomly, "Quent was way too excited to make you that coffee," and I realize how hard it will be to leave. To let go of this. Of everything I had wished for. But he smiles curiously, and I realize it would be far harder to stay.

"I want you to know that I'm proud. Of *The Passageway Plaza.* And what you got for it."

He shrugs. I am surprised he does not refuse this praise, does not shake his head or frown even.

"It was a materialistic goal, but anyway, I'm donating it all."

"You are?"

"Yup…to The Equal Justice Initiative. And The Sentencing Project."

"Really?"

"Yup."

"Hal."

"Yes?"

"I have to tell you something."

He sets his coffee down. "You already did," He says it with a sort of angst, as if knowing that I will be gone soon is enough for the day. But of course, there is more.

"I'm not a witch."

He leans back with his palms pressed to the ground, and grins as if I've made a joke. I look past him, at the empty room. The marble is in place and the books are stacked with purpose.

"I'm not a witch at all. I haven't...I haven't been doing anything for you. It's all been a coincidence. I made things happen for myself, that was true, but I never did anything for you. I couldn't possibly."

He shakes his head, his smile wiped. "But you did so much."

"I didn't, though."

"The Tarot card reading?"

"I know you better than you think."

"You think you do."

"You just think I don't."

"The awards? That event I escaped because of your trick with—"

"Your subconscious mind must have believed in what I said every time. Or you just trust me that much…so I got lucky. Every time."

There is a silence while he does not move and I cannot bear it.

"I'm sorry, Hal. I'm sorry that I lied and I'm sorry that I led you to believe something so untrue but it was the only way for me to get close to you. It was all just a way for me to know you."

"What?" He laughs, but it is not kind. "You wanted more fame? From spending time with me?"

"No. *No*, of course not. I knew before I got here that I disliked Hollywood, it's the reason I suffer for it now. But it was all—everything—everything happened this way just so that I could know you. I just needed a way—a path that would get me to you, and because you're famous, I had to become famous, too. Because the only thing I ever really wanted was you. To be with you. I have wanted you—to know you since before *Sailor's Siren*, and I'm sure that if you had never been discovered and I never even knew who you were, I would have gone my entire life without loving someone."

"Prisha," He says, and it sounds the same as when an adult says, "*child*". It is a tone that lacks reverence or sympathy. "You don't love me."

I shut my eyes.

"You don't know me enough to."

"I know you better than I know myself."

"No you don't. You don't mean anything you're saying. You are a witch, and you do not love me—"

"I'm *not*. I'm nothing. I can't do spells or grant your wishes or—"

"Stop saying that."

"—I can't. This entire time I was lying."

He shakes his head and breathes in sharply. "*Now* you're lying."

"I'm not."

"What about the letter? My *grand-mere*'s letter. What about that?"

"It was not my doing."

"It was."

"It was not."

"It had to have been. It was on my fucking desk, Prisha. In the middle of it. On top of all the other mail. I would have seen it long before that."

I place my hands above my head, run them through strands of misplaced hair. I hear myself apologize. I say I do not know how it happened. My voice is tired now. I am so tired.

"Why did I get everything I wanted this year, then? Huh? I've never—" He is doing it again. The stopping. The breathing.

I take the form from my bag. It is the first letter he ever mailed to me, the resignation contract. It is signed and sealed, it is done.

"I'll be gone by tonight."

He keeps his eyes on me, does not even glance at the papers. "You're leaving."

"I told you I was leaving."

He shakes his head as if I did not, but I did. I am sure I did.

"You're leaving because I proposed to Vivian. Because I'm getting married."

I flinch.

I do not speak.

I had not read the papers or watched the news. I could not bring myself to. Not when he is everywhere. Not when Hal's name and face is on *everything*.

So I did not know. I didn't know Hal was going to marry.

"You can't leave me—you can't just leave because I'm getting married."

My mouth wrinkles, and then I am crying. In the middle of his home, I cry. My shoulders shake and a jarring moan escapes me.

"You don't understand."

"I do understand," His voice is a whisper. My tears come hot and achingly quick. "You have no idea how much I do understand."

"But you don't, Hal. All my life—you are all I ever wanted."

He does not believe me still. His eyes shut and his head shakes with disbelief, but I do not bother giving him a story or a timeline. My tone is enough. If it did not sound so pained, then I would have told him about the first time I ever saw him, and the last. How from then to now, my feelings never faltered, but soared. Even now. *Even now.* They soar.

CHAPTER EIGHTEEN

Hal was fourteen years old when we first met. Four years before he would walk his first red carpet. Seven before we would meet again.

I was fourteen, too.

I had just missed the shuttle. It would not be much of a wait because it came around every ten minutes, but I was cold and the winters were not compassionate, so I walked home. My teeth gritted and the tip of my nose went red by the rub of my fingers and the dampness of my nostrils.

In school we learned the basics of Spanish, French, and English. Our principal was French but raised in America and most of the students spoke Spanish, so our instruction was a mix of languages. This is the reason why I understood what Hal's father said that day.

"*C'était à ta mère, tu ne vas rien lui dire.*"

Hal and I were the same height then.

He was scrawny and boyish and freshly mourning. In his hands was a pile of blue silk. Pale and clean, well kept and washed. I noticed this because the rest of him was the same way: clean.

Here, in East Rey, the people could not afford to be clean.

I kept walking, dirt lifting with every step I took. I tried to slow so that my tights would not grow grimy, but the wind ushered me forward. Hal's father cursed and I turned just barely, catching the glint of an empty bottle in his hands. A lick of brown liquid left.

"*I said no.*"

"*Elle est partie,*" Hal replied, and took long strides till he was standing beside me. It was then that I noticed the haze of gold around him. As if smushed there by finger, the color trailed around his body and caressed his face. "*She does not need it anymore.*" He said this to his father, over his shoulder.

I remember stepping away in my confusion, and wondering in the same moment if this boy is an angel.

He held the silk before my eyes. I did not take it, although I knew he wanted me to…It was tempting, this layer that could have saved me from falling ill, but I feared his father would get angry at me. Or worse, at Hal.

"Here," He said.

I felt my body inch forward and wondered mutedly if angels could be harmed.

My fingers wrapped around themselves. "I already have a scarf."

"But you are—" He frowned at me. "But you are cold."

"It's fine," I said, and thought, *this is the most beautiful boy that ever lived.* "Take it."

"My father will burn it one of these days. Take it, or it will be a waste."

I did not move, so Hal, ever so gentle, took my hand and placed the scarf there. I watched in awe as the gold lingered around my own skin. His father came from behind, grabbed Hal by his collar. Hal did not wince. He did not even blink.

"*Merci,*" I whispered, but it was too late. They were gone already, walking the opposite way, their voices harsh and mournful beneath the wind's cries. "*Merci.*"

★⁺₊★ ☾ ★⁺₊★

"I'm sorry." Hal stands. He walks over to Prisha. Places his arms around her, puts his face in her hair, and whispers words she thinks he does not mean. But he does.

"I'm sorry."

Prisha cries loudly, messily.

"I'm sorry. I love you, Sule. I'm sorry."

It is not the first time Hal has said he loves Prisha, but it is the first time he has said it to her.

She cries. She is limp in his arms.

"I'm sorry. I'm sorry. I love you so much, I love you."

"We had sex. And then I left, and I never went back."

"Had *what*?"

"We slept together."

"You and—Hal? Slept together? *When he'd just been engaged*?" Dustin could not hold back her shock—or disapproval—or excitement. She was all those things, at once.

"When you quit? *That night*?"

"Yes. I still don't have the words…to…to explain that."

Prisha's face shows no emotion, but she is thinking of that night now. She is thinking of bare freckled skin and newfound rhythms of breath. She is thinking of all that pain and all that pleasure. It had not been a surprise to feel that way. That was everything Hal had ever been to her, pain and pleasure.

HAL

When my père left, he did not say goodbye.

I remember this because it was the first time I realized there was something wrong with me.

Père had promised *maman* he would stay for me. Take care of me. It was the one thing she asked of him on her deathbed. He loved Haleena. It was the first thing I heard every rise of sun and moon, and yet he broke his promise to her. I had learned, with time, that I could not be loved for long.

The day after père left, *grand-mere* Chesca came to visit. She was not like the rest of The Moulins.

Chesca said a curse word in every sentence and preferred everything about France over America, except the music. She said "*bonswa*" in the mornings and divorced three times out of boredom. She was like my *maman*, but tougher. They shared cheekbones and an adoration for the arts. Chesca had modeled in her youth, too, and wrote for a hobby, but she never would have married an alcoholic.

It was December when she moved in, and the next morning, Chesca took me to my first acting audition. We stood in the hall beside fifteen other boys with the same brown head of hair as my own, and all I could think of was how my père had not said goodbye. Had not even left a note to explain.

He had left me.

Chesca must have known my thoughts, maybe she shared them, because she took my face in her calloused palms and spoke English for the first time that I'd ever heard.

"Your father…"

The door behind us pried open and a woman called my name. It was my turn, and I had not acted a day in my life.

"—is shit." Chesca let go of me and smiled. "Go, and *ne souris pas*."

I nodded and saw the satisfaction in her eyes as I stared back blandly. I was sure to show her that I would not smile like she had instructed me to, even when pleased.

From that moment on, everything I did was to impress *grand-mere* Chesca. It was my way of saying thank you and my way of trying to show her that I could be enough for her to stay, enough to be loved for long.

Chesca talked a lot, and I listened. She first told me about marriage. How every marriage, no matter what, would be warped in its own way. She said the rumors were true, man is from mars, and woman, from venus. She taught me how to embody equal amounts of femininity and masculinity and how I should never allow my face to give my feelings away—unless I was acting. She taught me to always treat everybody with respect, even if I did not feel like it. There was great power in that.

If I ever asked anything, ever wondered the veracity behind her teachings, she always had an answer.

I got the part, and then another. By my second role, there were billboards with my name on them and people asking for my signature even though I did not know cursive. It was not very long before I was the most famous actor of our time. The whole world would know my name, one way or another, by the time I turned 25 years old.

Before my first interview, Chesca patted my shoulders and said, "*ne souris pas*" again. She said this often to remind me of my desired persona. On the fifth interview, a month later, I smiled. I had met Vivian Astora. Her mothers were on-set and she had come with them. When I worked, I did not allow distractions. It was me and my role, that was all, but as I looked over at Chesca and saw the look of approval she wore, I wondered who it was for if not for me.

She had been looking at Vivian. The small-bodied, quiet blonde that kept her arms crossed over her chest. Chesca had told me that if I ever fell in love, it should be with someone who could live without me, or else they would prove themselves to be weak-minded and unreliable, like my *père*. So I dated Vivian.

We lived together for almost two years, the three of us. I drank black coffee throughout the day and read scripts. Vivian slept and baked and sang. She came home with a stereo one day, and from then on, we played old music and the rap my *grand-mere* liked.

Vivian never felt inclined to work and her mothers approved of that. Some days I watched as she slept in the backyard, her skin no longer pale but glowing beneath the sun's luster, and wondered if I should stop and join her in a life of perpetual nonchalance. But that never lasted long. All I had to do was look at Chesca, and suddenly I was working again.

My life was good. I did not think of *maman* and *père* much, which kept the grief at bay. I felt fine, until I did not anymore.

Chesca met Quent at a boxing match. She told me three things about the man. She trusted him, loved him, and he would be my bodyguard. I had nodded and listened, but felt frantic in those moments that she spoke of him.

Chesca would leave me, I knew it as she smiled and told me about the boxing match and the man who had won it. She felt weak being in love, and she could not bear to be weak.

Vivian grinned hearing of this, the stories of the handsome boxer who would have done anything to be with my *grand-mere*, but instantly I tasted bitter salt as I bit my tongue raw.

When Chesca left a week later, I did not cry. Vivian did. She had admired my *grand-mere* and did not understand why I shrugged rather than cry. But Chesca had put herself first, above everything and everyone else, and I understood that.

When I first met Prisha Sule, she reminded me of Chesca.

I was confused. Then intimidated. Sule was always one step ahead, thinking and planning and speaking. She had a set of eyes that were each reserved for a sole purpose.

The first, for her persona. A fabricated version of her; a more gentle and sprightly spoken female. She saw only her actions and the attention she received for them rather than the people who granted the attention itself. But not even I could disapprove of such self absorption; I paid even less attention than she to the people who put money in our pockets. In time, I found veneration for this specific part of Prisha, for the blatant fact that nothing could come between her and the goal which she aspired to accomplish.

The second eye is for me. Only me, merely me. Mine.

I did not even have to look her way in a room, I felt the energetic pull of her body positioned to face my own. To hear any sound I might utter. To descry any move I might make. Without this, I am nothing.

I met Sule when I was fourteen years old. At nineteen, we met again.

I won two Emmys that night. It had been sudden—the coincidental, effortless shift of my body, the turn that allowed me to catch sight of her—of Sule. I felt quick, overwhelming relief, and the photographers gave immortality to that look. It was the only photo of myself I could bear to look at for long. I had seen the girl from East Rey—no longer poor. No longer cold. No longer suffering. I felt drawn to speaking with her, compelled to ask what her life had been and become since we met, but then I heard the thrilled whispers among the crowd. And I was sure—absolutely—that I had been mistaken. This girl was said to be a witch. Born one. And so I turned my shoulder and told myself I had recognized her from a film, and that was all.

But then Quent came to me and asked, "Did you hear? A girl Lucy's agenting—Prisha Sule—she's a witch. I bet you can get her to manifest your Oscar for next year." He was joking, I think. But I had agreed and laughed, and suddenly six girls were put to the test.

After a month of working with Prisha, Quent came to me again. Shook his head and asked, "Are you in love with the girl?" I said no. Quent's head shook again.

"What?" I shrugged him off.

"How do you know I wasn't talking about Vivian?"

I did not reply. I blew the entire encounter off, until I could no longer. I was at home, Quent in the kitchen, the rest of the house emptied because she would arrive in minutes.

"How did you know?" I called.

I heard his laugh, dry and merciless from where I sat.

"Cause the house is quiet."

"That's because it was the one thing she asked of me."

"And the one thing you hate."

It was true. Silence had become anxiety inducing. If I could hear the fall of a penny then my palms would damp. My eyes would widen with alarm. *Maman* and *père* and Chesca had all left me, and I could not bear to be left alone in silence again.

I did not reply to Quent, but he knew.

I felt cruel, being with Vivian and thinking of Sule. I kept finding myself around her, beside her, inviting her over. I considered leaving Vivian, taking the loss of a family member just as I had many times before, but I remembered what Chesca had told me and knew I could never be with Sule. I would become weak with her, alive only in her presence, and she would leave me.

I accepted that we could not be and moved on—until Vivian told me she wanted kids.

"But we're twenty years old, Viv."

"My mom had me when she was twenty. So did yours."

"I just—now? Why right now?"

"I don't get it. *You* always told me you wanted kids. One boy, one girl—"

"But not at twenty, Viv. We're *kids* for god sake."

"We're adults, Hal. We've been together since we were kids."

"I just don't see why. Why now?"

"Because I want a family. What—do you not want one? Do you not want kids anymore?"

It was then that I knew, and perhaps Vivian too. I wanted kids, but not with her. Not with Vivian. She cried, and still I admitted to nothing.

The arguments were endless those two nights, and she cried till she fell ill. It was only a cold, but as she laid there, her skin reddened, eyes thick and flaky half in slumber, she whispered to me. Promised she would leave me and find somebody who would give her children, give her anything she asked for only because it was her who asked. Again, I was reminded that being alone was the worst thing I could bring to myself, and she knew. So I panicked and knelt at the bedside. Vivian and I married that Friday.

By Saturday afternoon, Prisha dropped her contract with Hyatt Blues and told Lucy Von Rage her "time was over long ago". Everybody came to me, telling me this as if they knew my mind. As if they knew what she was to me.

I went home where Vivian waited. It was midnight and she had been drinking. We both had.

She was still dressed, her white corset stained with fingerprints of wine and water.

We were not like before. We were distant and depressed and desperately affectionate with each other. But I decided it was all right, we had made a deal.

Marriage was a compromise; to never be alone and to have kids someday. So I made myself smile and moved forward to wipe away the wine from her gown.

"Don't."

"Don't what?"

"Don't touch me."

"What—why?"

Vivian was never one to smile in her anger, but she was different now. She smiled broadly, crookedly. "I married a man who loves another woman."

"You married me."

"*Exactly.*"

"You're crazy."

"No, you are—you're crazy for asking me to marry you. For thinking this would work while you're in love with that—"

"We made a deal."

"We made a promise, Hal. You promised you'd love me."

"I do love you."

"No. Not me. Not me." Vivian stood, took her glass of wine and stumbled down the hall. "You love her. You forget your eyes, Hal. They speak, too."

Years later, I would see that being alone was not the worst that could happen.

When Vivian finally left me, I did not feel much of anything. There was panic still—but fleeting and easily numbed.

I had people look into Prisha, try to find out where she was or what she was doing now, but she had always been very private, and more so since she'd left Hollywood.

It took years until somebody saw her again. She had married, but the man had taken her last name. So she stayed a Sule, and Santos joined her. Santos was three years older, grew up on the West Side of Rey, adopted at the age of fourteen by Laney and Oden Rue, two of the most well-paid directors in Hollywood. Even though he lived in the Hills, he still carried the neighborhood accent and drug addiction.

I wondered what Chesca would have thought of me, of who I had become. I only knew she would not be proud.

To be without Sule, I realized, was the saddest thing. I had never felt such sadness.

★⁺₊★ ☾ ★⁺₊★

The two women came forward, one in tears and the other stowing them away.

"How…how do you feel, now?" Dustin asks. She does not wipe away at the dampness. She encourages it.

She says, "After all this time. Are you…" Prisha drags a finger across her cheek and thinks that after all this time, *it is the same.* She thinks, *it has never changed.*

"I live a beautiful life."

"So you're happy, now?"

"I am. And I know what matters most, now, but Hal never went away." She taps her head, *here*, she means. "He never did."

"So—that's it? You never saw each other again?"

"Yes. It's been...almost thirty years."

The smoothies were long ago drained, the sunlight replaced with moonlight, seeping through the windows and onto the carpets.

"He never called? You didn't call? That...that was it?"

Prisha shrugs to herself.

"I left, and Benji came with me. He was seventeen and I had just gotten him a phone. I threw mine away because I was going mad waiting for a call. And then I married Santos Alvarez."

"The model? The guy who you went on the double date with?"

"Yes. He visited me in Solana often and then moved in for a few years. We got married, he wanted kids. I did too, but not...not with him...and then, that's all. I went back to Hollywood, once, for Nicolás' funeral. And Benji has his own place now, his own family. We still see eachother everyday."

"Nicolas?"

Prisha's face is a grimace. "May's Nicolás."

She pictures the last of what she saw of May.

A woman with dyed black hair, brittle in touch, and eyes that blinked too often in their loss. Her children were more of Nicolás than May, more frank and unshy, with his full cheeks and wide eyes. It is part of the reason she clings to them so miserably, stares at their faces as they hum in their slumber and weeps at the sight because she sees the boy she once knew.

"Do you think you'll ever meet again? You and Hal?"

Prisha opens her mouth, but the words do not come. She is quick to think *no*, but her mind is changed since meeting Dustin.

"Or talk, again? Not even see each other, just talk?"

"Now that I know about that portrait, I think so. I think maybe we will meet again."

Dustin does not say anything, but she is hoping, desperately, that they do.

There are more tears when she leaves. Dustin is thankful to this woman who has shown her what dreams are and how they do not need to be chased, but sworn by, and to leave when it is for your own good. Even when it leaves you an ache that will never wear off.

Dustin is sure that even now, if Hal were to repeat himself, Prisha would find the power to leave a second time, because she would put herself before everything else again if she had to.

They sip their teas and wipe their cheeks and Dustin goes home, to the massive house that is haunted by Prisha's love. She sits by the fireplace and imagines them in their youth. Hal and Prisha, grinning, sitting and speaking but holding back so much that forever stayed untold.

She falls asleep there, on a yarn rug beside the fire, and begins to picture something else as she falters.

She sees them no longer in their youth, their faces coming to a tiredness, marked with lines and gentle creases. She imagines them in the ways they would be if they left Hollywood together.

Them, on their way to another city, grinning with no regret. *Them*, in a cottage like Prisha's. *Them*, grasping each other's palms and speaking hushedly in a place that is half Paris and half forest.

Dustin's last thought is of Malena, the girl she has known since she was seventeen and watched with a spright longing since then. Dustin will tell her, she thinks, she will tell Malena before their time has run, too, and regret becomes so strong she will need to gasp for air, too. She will tell her everything.

THE END

      Hal Moulin and Prisha Sule are 49 years old when they meet again.

He is weary by then, driven restless by the fame, but more so from searching the ends of Earth just to find that Prisha was three hours away in Solana. *But she is here now*, he thinks, and cannot move his eyes from her in the rigid fear that she will be gone again. And this time, he will not be able to bear it. So he is standing, unblinking, and youth returns to his face.

Prisha bought the biggest property she could find in Solana. She never wore a scarf, she didn't have to. Her days went by spent at the seaside drinking from the bellies of coconuts, the other days spent in the backyard reading books that labeled her manifestation practices as "the law of attraction". When she opens the front door, two weeks upon meeting Dustin Bloom, Hal is waiting there. *Finally*, she thinks, *Finally.*

HAL

She is wearing a peach-colored dress. Her hair is brown now, cut above her shoulders and curling upwards. The third thing I see is the ring.

PRISHA

"*Hal*."

"Hi."

"Fuck, I'm in pajamas. How did—how did you find me?"

"I went to—" He starts, but doesn't finish. He is staring at my left hand. My ring finger.

"Hal?"

"You're still married."

I begin to nod, because technically, I am.

"To who?"

"To nobody."

"What?"

His hair is less curly now and drifting past his ears. He wears gray, all gray, and a single silver bracelet on his right hand. Hal was born with luck. Older now, but still has the fashioned beauty of a moviestar. There is no ring on his finger. I sigh at this.

"The divorce papers are being filed. So yes, legally I'm married, but The Who doesn't matter."

Hal's back begins to straighten again. He is shocked, maybe even hurt. I shake my head, *if only he knew*.

HAL

"Why?"

"Why, what?"

"Why did you divorce them?"

She smiles, no teeth, the flush of her lips pushing upward.

"What?" I ask, but I know she finds it amusing that I've assumed she was the one to divorce. But of course she was. Who the fuck would divorce Prisha Sule?

"Guess."

"Guess?"

"Yes, take a guess. I think you can figure it out."

"Just tell me," I am begging. "Tell me."

She nods, as if she will. And I nod too, to say something else, but I don't. I do not say that when she left all those years ago, I almost followed. That I drove to her house on the other side of the hills and planned to say, "I'm going with you." I do not say that the moment I got down on one knee, I regretted it. I do not say that I lived alone in the same home for two decades and it was all that I feared, but I would have done it all over again just to have this. To be here, now. And I do not tell her that all this time, I have done everything she ever taught me to one day meet again. I will tell her. Not now, but I will tell her one day.

PRISHA

At 14 years old, Hal Moulin was the reason for everything I ever did. I am almost 50 years old now, and Hal Moulin is still the goddamn reason.

"Would you like to come inside?"

"Yes. I would like to stay, actually."

"Okay."

"If you'll have me."

"I will," There is no hesitancy in me, no feigned nonchalance. "I'll have you."

"Alright," He walks the steps until he is standing before me, his eyes on mine. I have waited years to see them again. "I'm yours."

ACKNOWLEDGMENTS

★⁺₊★ ☾ ★⁺₊★

All of my gratitude is to you, Mom, for being the most lovely human there ever was. And to Dad, for being my best friend & sweetest supporter. I could not possibly tell you both how grateful I am & how deeply loved you are by me.

Most of this book was written by the poolside in Covina and a cafe on Castro street, but it is made up of every influence I've ever had. There are too many, but I'll start with the most powerful ones.

Thank you to both of my grandmas.

Grandma Chela, te adoro. Thank you Metztli, my confidant, and Moyo, for allowing me to type away while you slept. To my princesses: Leila, Desiree, Kimberly, Aubrey, for always making me feel loved. And to my entire family, all the Garcias & Tellez', for supporting me in all the ways you do.

So many thank yous to all of the invigorating programs &
mentors that got me to where I am, especially Ella from
GSP, Manny from the Youth Institute, and Rick from the
Boys & Girls Club.

Thank you to my closest friends, those who've shown me
genuine kindness and connection. My heart is possessed by
all of you. I am eternally appreciative of everybody who
has read my stories and manifestation articles, especially
Justin, whose comments and feedback are so cherished.

Thank you to all of the readers & writers that have
influenced me, all LOA coaches, and to anybody I've ever
said *I love you* to…I say it so rarely because I mean it so
deeply.

I am forever thankful for you.

About the Author

★⁺₊★ ☾ ★⁺₊★

Manauia was born and raised in East Los Angeles but currently lives in San Francisco pursuing a BA in Creative Writing. *The Witch of Hollywood* is her second book, but the first published. She writes short stories and manifestation guides on her website: manauiawrites.com.

Instagram: @manauiia

Made in the USA
Las Vegas, NV
05 December 2022

61254449R00233